I0715917

CARPE MAÑANA

the publishing CIRCLE™

CARPE MAÑANA
FIRST EDITION
ISBN 978-1-955018-50-0 (HARDCOVER)
ISBN 978-1-955018-53-1 (PAPERBACK)
ISBN 978-1-955018-56-2 (LARGE-PRINT PAPERBACK)
ISBN 978-1-955018-59-3 (E-BOOK)

Book design by Michele Uplinger

CARPE MAÑANA

A NOVEL

JOE S. BULLOCK

PRAISE

Joe Bullock's *Carpe Mañana* is a wonderful, heartfelt character driven story. It's not often we get a gripping story with rich, deep characters. This is one of those books. Joe's narrative style moves the reader along while pulling at our heartstrings. It showcases the people and landscape of New Mexico, fully exploring the "Land of Enchantment" in all its majestic glory. I highly recommend this book to anyone who wants to feel good. So often we are subjected to negativity and bad news. Joe Bullock's book is a welcome respite from that. It is uplifting, fun and funny. It's hard to put down. I was sad when it was over. But glad I had the chance to visit with the terrific, well-written characters and feel-good story.

ROSS MARKS
AWARD-WINNING FILMMAKER / PROFESSOR, NEW MEXICO STATE UNIVERSITY

A compelling heartwarming story of love, faith and divine intervention set into today's chaotic environment. A must read for those contemplating "Esperanza por el future"—"Hope for the future."

DANIEL E DUGGAN, COLONEL (RET.) USA

Carpe Mañana is an uplifting novel of faith readers can seize today. Those who have read Bullock's first novel, *Walking With Herb*, or who have seen the excellent motion picture with the same title, will recognize familiar themes of faith, trust, and perseverance.

JIM HARRIS
AUTHOR OF TWO DOZEN BOOKS / LONG-TIME NEWSPAPER JOURNALIST

What Joe Bullock accomplished with his incredible *Walking With Herb* novel, he has surpassed with *Carpe Mañana*. A compelling story of people's lives who have encountered overwhelming tragedies, culminating in a beautiful spiritual ending, leading readers to trust and love God through the Lord Jesus Christ.

BERT WIMBERLY
SENIOR PASTOR AND FOUNDER, GATES OF THE CITY CHURCH
KERRVILLE, TEXAS

Many are familiar with the Horace phrase "Carpe Diem", (Seize the Day!) I had never heard of the great poet's command being applied to the future, as Joe Bullock so adroitly did, with the title of his new book. *Carpe Mañana* is an exciting sequel to Bullock's *Walking With Herb*, published in 2016, and subsequently made into a major movie in 2020. He again weaves his magical storytelling into a book that touches on loss, faith, finding love, systemic societal issues, and finally a choice for individuals to "seize tomorrow." This uplifting book reminds readers that God has a plan for each of us, and that caring for and loving each other are integral parts of the plan—good things do happen to good people.

KENNETH J. FERRONE
EXECUTIVE DIRECTOR OF CATHOLIC CHARITIES OF SOUTHERN NEW MEXICO

Joe Bullock, in his new book, *Carpe Mañana*, follows the style and theme of his successful book, *Walking With Herb*, as it also reveals the influence of the Lord in affecting and directing the lives of the characters. The book is an easy, great read . . . exciting, occasionally suspenseful, with a very uplifting outcome for the good guys. Once you start this book, it is hard to put it down!

GARREY CARRUTHERS
FORMER GOVERNOR OF NEW MEXICO

After a riveting prologue in the jungles of Vietnam, Joe Bullock weaves a present-day story of triumph and redemption, featuring two engaging protagonists, a man and a woman, plus a mysterious figure who helps each of them find their way back to God. Setting his book in the splendor of the high desert mountains, Bullock addresses troubling personal and societal issues with his customary blend of wisdom, humor, and profound spirituality.

THE REVEREND DR. JEANNE LUTZ

To my loving, supporting, wife of 41 years, Sheila.
Everyone should have a wife like Sheila,
a mother like Sheila,
grandmother like Sheila,
and a friend like Sheila.
She is a blessing to all who know her.

ACKNOWLEDGMENTS

'M NOT A FULL-TIME WRITER. AS SUCH, THE ORIGINAL drafts of my manuscripts are rather amateurish. Thank goodness, I've had help! My late friend, Tony Award Winner Mark Medoff, best known for penning *Children of a Lesser God*, provided invaluable mentoring. Mark and his son-in-law, Ross Marks, transformed my first novel, *Walking with Herb*, into a wonderful movie of the same name. I owe a great debt to them, as well as to my generous friends who invested their money to bring the movie to life.

I believe that God led me to Linda Stirling as my publisher for *Carpe Mañana*. This springs from my belief that God is constantly guiding us with signs, which we too often mis-interpret as merely coincidences. In July of 2023, my wife and I were on a flight to Portland to celebrate the 50th wedding anniversary of close friends. I was seated next to a young lady who was reading a medical manual. Very rarely do I strike up a conversation with my fellow passengers. I normally give a polite greeting and settle in to either read a book or take a nap. On this occasion, I decided to ask her about the material she was reading. I am on the board of directors of a local hospital and have a keen interest in medical issues. Our conversation morphed into a light chat about our personal lives. I told her that I had written a spiritual book, which became a movie, and was currently working on another book, but not sure about using the same publisher. Turned out, she is Linda's daughter. She told me about her mother's publishing company, The Publishing Circle. The more she told me about her mother's company, the more I became convinced that Linda would be a great fit for my new book. After contacting her, I knew I had found the right person. The result has been a great collaboration, for which I am both blessed and grateful.

Many thanks to Claudia Saenz Clements, for helping this techno-challenged writer with numerous computer-related problems. We invented a new Spanish word for the process: "Claudiadarme," por favor?

Finally, I want to acknowledge how blessed I am to have my twin brother, Van Bullock, as my best friend. My old "wombmate" has always had my back.

CARPE
MAÑANA

Prologue

Jim Viejo
QUANG NAM, VIETNAM, SEPTEMBER 1971

THE JUNGLE SEEMED UNNATURALLY QUIET. NO CALLS from screeching birds or shrieks from disturbed monkeys filled the air. No loud cracks from M-16 rifles reverberated through the dense vegetation of the jungle understory. The only sounds 1st Lieutenant James Viejo could hear were his heart beating in his ears and the gentle scrunch of his footfall as he led the patrol deeper into enemy territory. He and his men were taking part in Operation Lan Son 810, a counter-offensive meant to disrupt North Vietnamese efforts to make further inroads to the south. Quang Nam's central location just west of the Laos border made it easy for both the North Vietnamese Army and the Viet Cong to launch probing thrusts to determine South Vietnamese troop strength and positions. The mission of Operation Lan Son 810 was to reduce the frequency of enemy incursions into the area.

Viejo, in the point position, raised his left hand above his head to signal the twelve men in his squad to halt. Something didn't feel right. He'd learned long ago on his first tour in Nam with the 3rd Marine Amphibious Brigade that the VC were crafty little bastards, capable of just about anything that would kill American soldiers—the sneaky placement of feces-coated punji sticks or bouncing Betties that popped up from spring-loaded mechanisms designed to get the explosives to chest level where the blasts would do the most damage.

"What's up, Jim?" whispered gunnery sergeant Ross Marks, a tall, skinny black kid from Detroit.

"Dunno," Viejo whispered back. "Something's wrong. I can feel it."

Taking a deep breath to slow his heart rate, Viejo relaxed his grip on the stalk of his M-16, feeling the sweat pour over his face and stream down his back. The seasonal monsoon had begun in June, and it was now in full force in September. As if on cue, thunder rumbled in the distance, adding to the feeling of impending doom surfacing in Viejo's consciousness. He'd developed a sixth sense over his months in combat, and it was telling him the danger was mounting by the minute, though he couldn't identify the source. *Something bad was about to happen!*

Viejo cursed his bad luck. In April, the majority of the Marine Corps had bugged out of Nam as part of the major drawdown of United States forces in accordance with the Pentagon's plan to Vietnamize the war effort. The Vietnamese would have to shoulder the burden of settling the score with their northern neighbors. Fewer than five hundred Marines remained in-country, and most of them were in arms support or advisory positions.

Viejo's squad was in the field on a special assignment to assist in the execution of Operation Lan Son 810, a dubious honor at best and a possible punishment from his commanding officer at worst. Viejo knew the CO hated him. Early on his arrival, Viejo had called him out at a staff meeting about a poor command decision that had resulted in unnecessary casualties. Viejo realized his inability to hold back his opinions over his career had cost him the promotions he thought he richly deserved. Hell, he should've been a captain or a major after nearly completing two combat tours, particularly given the fact that the life expectancy of lieutenants in hot zones usually wasn't very long.

Viejo moved slowly forward, every sense on high alert. Rain beat a steady patter on the thick, almost impenetrable rainforest canopy. The sound of thunder grew louder.

Just what we don't need, Viejo thought.

Viejo continued to advance until the jungle foliage thinned and more light penetrated the canopy. Ahead, he saw the open expanse of a rice paddy and an adjacent village with the usual thatched-roof shacks, pigsties, and chicken coops. Men, women, and children dressed in shabby black clothing went about their business. All looked peaceful and normal. Viejo wasn't buying it. Villages like the one he was now watching were hotbeds for the VC. The citizens often lent the invaders their support despite dire consequences if the Americans found out. They likely figured that the VC would be around long after the Americans left, and it wouldn't go well for anyone who aided the Americans.

Signaling his men to follow, Viejo carefully inched out of the jungle onto more open ground. He hunched down in the tall grass extending above his shoulders and lifted his field glasses to his eyes. Seeing nothing suspicious, he stood up and continued to move through the grass. Gunnery Sergeant Marks advanced at his side.

"Seems like everything's okay," Marks said, keeping his voice low.

"Yeah, it does. That's what bothers me."

"We gonna search the village?"

"That's why we're here. Need to find any useful information," Viejo replied. "We'll go in. Take a look—"

The unmistakable thump and whoosh of an incoming mortar round stopped Viejo in mid-sentence.

"Incoming!" he screamed, diving for cover.

The mortar round exploded a hundred yards short of them. The gunners obviously hadn't quite gotten the range right, but Viejo knew it would only be a matter of minutes before they did. Other incoming rounds followed, sending dirt, rocks, and vegetation flying amid acrid gray and black smoke. Machine gun and small arms fire erupted all around them. Viejo realized he'd led his men right into an ambush. He scanned the surrounding terrain and noted the positions of the muzzle flashes.

Turning to his men, he shouted, "Fall back! Fall back to the jungle! Marks and Diego, lay down suppression fire to give us cover!"

Marks dropped to a prone position alongside Diego and returned the enemy fire. Viejo added his firepower to give the rest of the squad time to retreat. As he fired, he felt the disturbed air near his right cheek as a round passed close to the side of his head. Smoke obscured his vision. The cacophony of exploding mortars and guns firing made his ears ring.

A large number of Viet Cong troops burst from the tall grass, their guns blazing. Grenades exploded, sending shrapnel tearing into several of his men. He looked to the left and saw Marks writhing in agony. The explosion tore through his arms and chest, peppering him with white-hot shards of sharp metal. Blood was soaking the ground around him as he screamed in pain.

"Medic! Medic!" Viejo shouted, rushing to Marks's side. "I got you, man! Everything's gonna be okay! You hear me? Stay with me, Ross! Stay with me, brother!"

The medic rushed to help as the enemy fire increased, getting closer.

"Get the hell out of here!" Viejo yelled to Diego. "I got Marks! *Go! Go! Go!*"

Diego sprinted toward the edge of the jungle just as a mortar round struck. A geyser of black dirt erupted amidst the bright orange fireball that enveloped Diego, vaporizing the lower half of his body and killing him instantly.

Viejo realized they were pinned down, outmanned, and outgunned. If they stayed, they'd die. He didn't think they stood much of a chance in the jungle, either. Chances were good that enemy reinforcements were advancing on their position.

Marks no longer screamed in agony. The morphine the medic administered had kicked in and he merely moaned. It pained Viejo to see his friend cut to ribbons like that, and the anger in him blossomed anew. If he could kill every last one of the VC, he would, and he'd enjoy doing it.

Viejo crawled to the radioman and told him to call in air strikes to lay down a carpet of napalm.

"We'll burn their sorry asses!" he yelled over the din of battle. "Get a medivac in here now!"

The radioman got through to the forward operating base as more VC poured out of the jungle behind them.

Crap! Viejo thought as he jammed another magazine into his M-16.

He signaled his men to consolidate their position as they moved to form a rough circle to provide suppression fire on all sides. He thought of the Alamo, a place he'd visited as a kid after watching the Disney movie on TV. The image of Davey Crocket and Jim Bowie fighting off hordes of attackers came and went in a flash. It struck him that he and his squad were trapped in a similarly dire situation.

Two F-100 Super Sabre fighter jets roared overhead, circled wide, and dropped a series of napalm bombs exploding in sheets of fire on the enemy positions. The ground shook with each impact. Enemy fire continued, though thank God it became more and more sporadic. Viejo heard the thump-thump-thump of incoming copters, feeling a surge of relief as he released a smoke bomb to mark their position.

The choppers strafed the tall grass and surrounding jungle, circling twice before coming in hot, the .50-cals blazing, blue smoke and orange flames at the muzzle, bands of bright green tracer rounds marking the trajectory of fire down range. Thick, black, oily smoke from the napalm filled the air, partially obscuring the Marine's evacuation from the enemy guns and allowing the men to sprint toward the choppers with less chance of being hit.

"Hold on, Ross," Viejo said. "Stay with me! We got your six."

Viejo helped the medic carry Marks to the chopper under withering machine guns and small arms fire. Sparks flew off the chopper as enemy rounds peppered its side. He jumped into the bay and pulled Marks in.

"Go, go, go!" Viejo screamed.

The pilot pulled back on the yoke, and the chopper rose quickly. Viejo watched the ground recede, the white-yellow blink of muzzle flashes clearly indicating enemy positions. Two more Super Sabres roared in, this time dropping explosive munitions instead of napalm. It seemed clear to Viejo that he'd walked into a sizeable force. They were lucky that any of them had survived.

A few minutes later, the noise of battle faded as the helicopter flew over the jungle canopy toward the forward operating base and field hospital. It always struck Viejo as strange, the feeling of peace and serenity that came over him after a battle, likely the result of adrenalin withdrawal. He gazed out the bay at the endless green of the jungle and wondered if his ticket would get punched before he got the hell out of Dodge, and, at that point, was too tired to give it much consideration. Running on empty, he didn't know how much more he had to give. One thing was certain, though. He'd never let his men down. He'd never let them down, no matter what, even if he got killed in the process.

1

Viejo

CAMP PENDLETON
OCEANSIDE, CALIFORNIA
APRIL 29, 2004

THE SMELL OF SALT CARRIED ON THE PACIFIC OCEAN breeze wafting through his open bedroom window did not invigorate Colonel James Viejo. No, not on this particular morning, with the prospect of the odious task he and the base chaplain would face in the coming hours. The beautiful spring weather belied the fact that the war in Iraq continued with no end in sight. His fellow Marines were fighting insurgents, casualties occurring on a daily basis. Continuing evidence of the fact that humans are, by and large, a poorly evolved species. God's grand design, for some strange reason, included humanity, but for the life of him, Viejo didn't understand why. It didn't seem right that the people who want and seek power are exactly the kind of people who shouldn't have power.

He thought about that as he stood at the bathroom sink in his white boxer shorts, still groggy from a fitful night's sleep. Was there any good in him? If so, how could he have spent much of his career training newly minted Marines in the art of combat, which, in reality, was the art of killing? Were he and the men he trained, killers or merely optionless weapons? In the courtroom of his mind, he could make his case that he had no choice but to carry out orders coming down from political leaders . . . leaders who, for the most part, definitely were not good people, caring only about their political ambitions, with no concern about the human misery entailed. Once again, for at least the thousandth time, he couldn't win his case. The prosecutor in his mental courtroom would present the same damning, irrefutable evidence of his guilt. "If you were merely an innocent tool, Viejo, why did God punish you by taking your wife?"

Viejo had no response. Betti, his beloved wife, had died of a sudden and aggressive form of cancer five years ago, slamming the door on his ability to ever again experience the joy provided by his soulmate. Having proven him guilty on the first count of killing other human beings, his prosecutor moved to count two: the sin of training others to kill.

"Your Honor, the evidence here is even stronger, as the punishment meted out by God fits the sin so well! The defendant's own son, Michael Viejo, suffered the same fate as the young men who died in combat after the defendant trained them and sent them to fight!"

Vivid memories from the worst day of his life flooded into Viejo's mind as he stared numbly into the deep recesses of the mirror.

Michael, also a Marine, had advanced with his squad in the 1st Marine Division north-westward up the Tigris-Euphrates River Valley in March 2003. They took heavy fire in pockets where the Republican Guard put up a stiff fight. Viejo recalled watching the news on CNN and wondering where Michael was and what he was doing. If he were okay, or if he'd been killed or wounded. His dear friend, Ross Marks, had recovered from his injuries sustained in Nam. Upon returning stateside, Marks entered Officer Training and advanced rapidly through the ranks, getting his Star last year. Marks had recently been assigned the command at Camp Pendleton. Out of respect for their friendship, he gave Viejo as much inside information about Michael as he could, but there was no way of knowing exactly what Michael's individual status was. Although Viejo was a hardened combat vet, he was a dad with all the love a good parent felt for his child. He worried himself sick about Michael, especially when the news showed the American army and Marine forces fighting it out on the streets of Baghdad in early April.

When his CO called him into his office, face grim, hands folded in front of him as he sat behind his cluttered desk, Viejo's heart sank. General Marks didn't have to spell it out with words. His sad eyes said it all.

"Sit down, Jim," General Marks said, his voice low and full of emotion. "I have some terrible news about Michael."

Viejo sat down, his hands shaking, his heart racing. He had known right away that something was horribly wrong and that it had to do with Michael before his friend even spoke.

General Marks proceeded to tell him that Michael died from sniper fire on the streets of Baghdad on April 9, the same day the city fell, and Basra to the south surrendered to British forces. The news hit Viejo hard, causing him to break down in front of Marks.

"I, I can't believe God has taken him from me," Viejo said, wiping tears from his eyes. "First Betti and now my son. Why is He punishing me?"

"I'm so sorry, Jim," Marks said. "Why don't you take some time to get your head around all this? Maybe talk to the chaplain."

"I don't want to talk to the chaplain. I'm not really into God at the moment," Viejo said, standing up from his chair. "He damn sure isn't into me!"

Viejo's deep despair gave way to anger.

"Don't say that," Marks said. "You're not yourself right now. And why would you be?"

General Marks stood up from his desk, came around it, and gently gave Viejo a hug. Then he stepped back.

"Come on," he said, "let's get out of here. Let's get some fresh air."

" No. Thanks. I really don't want to be with anybody, not even you."

In the year since Michael's death, the pain had not abated. If anything, it continued to metastasize like cancer, eating into his sanity. He doubted the possibility of recovery. He gradually atrophied into a hollowed-out version of his former self, trying to survive with a lot of help from valium and booze.

His hands shook as he opened the medicine cabinet, took the pill bottle from the shelf, opened it, and tapped several pills into his left palm. He stared at them for a long moment, wondering how he'd fallen so far and seemingly so fast. Viejo knew Betti would be very disappointed in him as he popped the pills, swallowing them dry, chasing them with a couple of gulps of water from the tap.

He splashed cold water on his face and looked in the mirror. The face looking back at him, once ruggedly handsome, reflected fifty-eight years of hard use. Deep creases appeared on his weathered, tanned cheeks, and streaks of white mingled with lighter gray sprinkled his formerly jet-black hair. Deep brown eyes provided portals to the torture behind them. In contrast to his weary visage, Viejo's taut, muscular physique remained in superb shape. He had maintained a strict regimen of physical training throughout his career, increasing the intensity of his workouts over recent months in an attempt to divert a portion of his anger-driven energy. Endorphins released by the vigorous physical activity provided him a modicum of temporary relief.

Sighing, he took the toothbrush from the glass on the sink, applied a dab of toothpaste, and began to methodically brush his teeth. He was like that, methodical in routine matters. The regimentation of military life generally creeps over into one's personal habits. Finished brushing his teeth, went back into the bedroom and donned his dress blues. He checked his watch, noting that the driver would arrive with the chaplain in a few minutes, and left the apartment to wait outside.

Viejo took several deep breaths to calm his nerves. He gazed up at the intensely blue cloudless sky, and, for just a few moments, his pain and anxiety diminished as the pills did their trick. He'd been stationed at Marine Corps Base Camp Pendleton in Oceanside, California, for twelve years now. When he and Betti first arrived, he couldn't believe their good luck with the new duty station just thirty-eight miles from the beautiful city of San Diego.

The largest expeditionary training base on the West Coast at about 125,000 acres, the natural beauty of the facility had impressed them both from the start. In his off hours, he and Betti explored the beaches, bluffs, mesas, canyons, and mountains in what he surprisingly learned was the largest undeveloped portion of coastline in Southern California. Life on the base had been almost blissful until Betti got sick and died. After her death, loneliness swept in, despite the fact that the base was home to thirty-eight thousand military families.

A few minutes later, a civilian black sedan pulled up, and Viejo got in. He exchanged somber greetings with the driver and the chaplain.

Viejo and the Chaplin Knorr were being driven to Barstow to deliver the awful news to the wife of Sargent David R. Medina, that her husband had been killed in action.

"Shouldn't be too much traffic on the way to Barstow," he said, making himself comfortable as the car pulled away.

"Hope not," Chaplain Knorr said. "Although, I'd give anything not to have to do this."

"Yeah, me too," Viejo said.

He read the file detailing Medina's personal profile and realized the dead Marine was the same age as Michael was when he was KIA. The pain instantly intensified as he internalized how the young wife was going to react when he told her that her husband was killed in an ambush outside a small Iraqi village. The poor woman was only twenty-three with two kids, a three-year-old daughter, and a one-year-old son. War's consequences bite deep, particularly in military families. Civilian families, for the most part, go about daily life without giving much thought to the sacrifices others were making on their behalf.

Viejo fell silent, glad that Chaplain Knorr didn't feel like talking either. The rest of the ride passed in gloomy contemplation and dark thoughts of death. The faces of men he'd lost in combat flashed before him. He squeezed his eyes closed to force them away. Stabs of familiar guilt tore through him when he considered that he'd not only killed, a definite violation of one of the most important of the Ten Commandments, but he'd also trained others to kill as well. He felt he was part of the problem, and part of the making of the misery that Catherine Medina was about to experience in spades.

Traffic was light, and they arrived at the Medina residence at roughly 0930. The Medina family lived in a rundown old apartment building in a seedy part of town, obviously the best they could afford. Low military pay had long vexed Viejo. Was it fair to send soldiers into harm's way with such small compensation? The pay was so small; many families of enlisted personnel were on food stamps. Viejo could see no justice or fairness. Not one bit. He'd pushed for change and got in trouble for his efforts. Eventually, he resigned himself to the fact that one man couldn't influence institutions.

Glancing over at Chaplain Knorr, Viejo sighed, "Well, guess we should get this over with."

"I really hate death notice duty. It's one of the hardest parts of the job."

"Tell me about it," Viejo said, opening the car door.

He got out of the car and put his cap on. Together, he and the chaplain entered the apartment building and rode the elevator up to the fourth floor. His heart began to beat faster when they reached the door. He took three deep breaths to calm down.

"Breathing exercises," he said, nodding toward his companion. "A shrink friend of mine told me about them a few years back. Said they do wonders when you're stressed out."

"Well, do they? Do wonders, I mean?"

"Yes, and no. Today, I don't think anything'll help."

Viejo pressed the door buzzer and held his cap over his heart. He heard footsteps. The door was opened by a petite brunette with piercing brown eyes. She cradled an infant boy in the crook of her right arm. The second she saw them, she gasped.

"Mrs. Medina," Viejo asked, "may we come inside?"

The woman immediately became distraught. *"Oh, my God! No! No! No!"*

Viejo's heart broke for her and her children. The daughter would soon forget what her father looked and sounded like. He would fade away in her mind as time passed and as her mom moved on to a new life. The little boy wouldn't even possess a memory of his dad. It would be almost as if his father had never existed at all. Another brutal consequence of war.

"I'm afraid Sergeant Medina was killed in action two days ago during a firefight outside a small Iraqi village," Viejo said. "I'm so, so sorry for your loss."

Mrs. Medina turned away from them and put the baby in a bassinet in the living room. She collapsed on the sofa, buried her head in both hands and sobbed uncontrollably. "This can't be! David was due to come home next month. He has never seen David Jr. This isn't happening."

Viejo, on the verge of tears, could barely respond. "I'm sorry. His death was confirmed by the surviving members of his unit; there's no chance of an error. His personal effects are being sent to Pendleton. We will get them to you as soon as possible."

"Mommy?" the little girl said, her voice shaky, "what's the matter? What's wrong?"

Chaplain Knorr sat down next to Mrs. Medina and put his arm around her shoulder. She leaned into his chest and sobbed.

"I'm so sorry," Chaplain Knorr said as he gently rubbed her back. "Is there someone we can call for you?"

"Mommy? What's going on?" the little girl persisted, becoming increasingly agitated with every passing second.

"Your daddy's gone to heaven," Mrs. Medina cried.

"What do you mean?"

Chaplin Knorr knelt in front of her, put both hands on her shoulders, and said, "Sometimes God calls people to Him sooner than what we want or expect. Your daddy's with God now."

The little girl began to cry. She ran to her mother, and they embraced amid sobs that threatened to wrench Viejo's heart right out of his chest. The sound of utter grief and shock in the voices of the survivors when first hearing that their loved one had been killed in action always hurt the most, struck deep, reopening his personal wounds.

Viejo stood up and glanced at Chaplain Knorr.

"Do you have someone to come over and help? We can stay with you until they get here," the chaplain offered.

Mrs. Medina looked up at them, the grief so clear on her face that Viejo tapped right into it, spurring his own dark emotions. Doing death duty notice always triggered him, and, for a moment, he wondered if his immediate commanding officers gave him the assignment to make him feel even more uncomfortable with his position in the Marines, hoping it would drive him to retire. Lately, he'd been getting the distinct impression that his career was pretty much over whether he wanted it to be or not.

"I just want to be alone," she said between sobs. "Go away. Get out! *Get out!*"

Her reaction didn't surprise Viejo. Typically, denial quickly dissolved into rage.

"Okay then," Viejo said. "Again, I'm so sorry for your loss."

The words sounded as hollow to him as they always did. But really, what else could be said at a time like this?

Putting his cap back on, Viejo turned to Chaplain Knorr. "Come on, let's go."

He turned away from the grieving widow and they walked out the door, closing the door gently behind him.

2

Renee Romero
PRESENT TIMES

DISTRICT JUDGE RENEE ROMERO FELT CERTAIN OF THE jury's verdict as she took her seat behind the bench. The gangbanger in question, Bernardo Espinoza, was on trial for kidnapping and raping a teenage girl before she managed to escape and call the police. He was picked up at his usual haunt, a bar in the barrio known for its criminal activity, chiefly drug sales and prostitution, and brought to the precinct, where he was charged and booked. Denied bail, he'd been cooling his jets in county jail for seven months while awaiting trial. His defense attorney claimed the court violated Espinoza's right to speedy justice. He raised all kinds of a big stink about it, although the long wait time was nothing out of the ordinary, par for the course in a justice system clogged with a never-ending backlog of cases waiting to be heard.

Romero considered the defense attorney's assertion frivolous and irrelevant. The argument merely reinforced her inner sense of discontentment with the profession as a whole. At fifty-five, Romero had been around the block a few times. She figured she'd seen it all by now, but she also knew trial outcomes were unpredictable, as juries often rendered verdicts frequently populated with individuals who were ignorant of the laws and legal procedures. Juries were commonly compromised of tampered jurors who had been bribed or threatened. Many citizens surmise that juries aren't the smartest folks around, because in general, smart people can figure out a way to avoid jury duty. Jury selection is one of the first components of a trial, and the process itself generally does not result in the generally believed "jury of one's peers" concept proposed by our forefathers. The selection process itself is skewed, as lawyers on both sides maneuver to weigh the jury with jurors prejudiced to their desired verdict.

Feeling confident about the outcome, Romero asked the forewoman if the jury had reached a verdict.

"We have, Your Honor," the forewoman said. "We, the jury, find the defendant, Bernardo Espinoza, not guilty."

Romero was thunderstruck. She absolutely couldn't believe what she'd just heard.

How could these idiots put a monster like that back out on the streets? she fumed. *Little wonder that the gangs are out of control in the city if a clear-cut case like this can't get justice!*

Romero took small comfort seeing that the spectators evidently agreed with her, or at least most of them did. They groaned and shouted in protest. The victim bowed her head and began to cry. Her mother gently rubbed her back. Nick Hemphill, the prosecutor, looked as stunned as Romero. The defense attorney beamed and slapped Espinoza on the back, receiving a high-five from the gangbanger in return. It sickened Romero to see them celebrating, but she was powerless to do anything about it. She certainly couldn't overrule the verdict.

"Order in the court!" she shouted as she banged her gavel three times. "Order! Order in the court!"

Everyone went silent. Romero heard the victim's soft crying, adding to her frustration and anger over the injustice that had just been done.

"I want to thank the jury for your service," Romero said. She turned to face Espinoza and said, "Mr. Espinoza, you are free to go, but I suspect you'll be back . . . soon."

The gangbanger just grinned as he and his attorney stood up from the defense table. The victim and her mother stood up with the prosecutor. Romero heard him apologizing to her. Sick with fury, Romero stood and left the courtroom, storming back to her chambers, where she immediately hung up her robe and poured herself a few fingers of scotch from the bottle she kept in a filing cabinet next to her desk.

A few minutes later, her door opened without a knock. Nick, the young prosecutor, accompanied by the bailiff, Daniel Payne, stormed into the room. Clearly, they shared her anger about the verdict.

Romero took another long pull from her glass of scotch as they sat down in the chairs in front of her desk. Nick looked like his dog had just died.

"I can't believe they let the scumbag off," Nick whined.

"I thought for sure they'd convict," Payne added.

"I thought so too," Romero replied as she fought to remain professional in front of her colleagues.

"You know, Your Honor, I thought I had this case nailed," Nick continued. "If I can't get a conviction in an open-and-shut case like this, maybe I'm in the wrong profession. I mean, who would have thought that the jury would ignore all the overwhelming evidence and let the guy skate off to find more victims?"

"You can cut the 'Your Honor' crap, Nick. We're not in the courtroom," Romero replied. "This isn't the first time something like this has happened, and it damn sure won't be the last. It damn sure wasn't your fault! You did an excellent job presenting the people's case against Espinoza, just as you did in the mock trials back in law school when you were one of my top students. It's not your fault that our legal system is sick, infected by the corruption and moral decay creeping in from society in general. You guys go have a couple of drinks down at the Two Fools Tavern. Shake this off, and be ready to come in to work Monday, for another full week of batting our heads against the wall."

The two men said their goodbyes, wearily rose to their feet, and trudged out the door. Romero sipped on her scotch. As the soothing effect of the alcohol quieted her nerves, she drifted into a state of philosophical contemplation. How did she arrive at this point? Her discontent with the legal system had been simmering for years, especially recently. Was she imploding, in sync with the imploding system? It wasn't always that way. Back when she graduated from law school at the University of New Mexico, like many newly minted attorneys, she had looked at the world through rose-colored glasses. She thought she could be a force for good, for positive change, and she especially wanted to make a difference in her beloved home city of Albuquerque. She grew up in a primarily low-income Hispanic neighborhood, along with her five siblings. Her father was Hispanic. Her mother was as Irish as you can get. Both were public school teachers. Devoutly Catholic, they practiced the rhythm method, predictably leading to a family of six children. Her father had often joked that two of the basic tenets of the Catholic Church were rhythm and bingo. If your rhythm was off a little, then bingo! As educators, her parents emphasized school above everything other than the Church. After graduating with honors from the University of New Mexico, she excelled at law school.

Her first job out of law school was a junior position with the District Attorney's office. Although the salary was meager, the job provided substantial hands-on trial experience, unlike private firms wherein the partners handled the trial work, with the younger associates doing mainly research and interviewing.

Realizing that as her parents aged, they would likely need financial assistance, she left her position as a junior attorney in the prosecutor's office to work at a private law firm. This was not an uncommon occurrence. The private firms would let the DA's office provide young lawyers with training and trial experience, then lure them away with much better salary offers. Not long after joining the firm, she met the man she thought would be her prince charming. He had just made partner in the law practice. Although several years older than Renee, he was virile and wonderfully charming. Together, they made quite the power couple. Their marriage lasted for two decades, until her husband fell for his gold-digging assistant, a little blonde, eighteen years his junior. He had taken off with her five years ago, filing for divorce in the process. Initially, she'd been devastated, but, over time, she came to realize that he'd probably been cheating on her during their entire marriage. The love she thought they'd shared existed only in her imagination. It probably also explained why he was adamant about not having children.

Shortly after her divorce, her uncle, a district judge, retired after a sudden illness. He was well-respected and able to have her appointed to fill out his term. When the term ended, she ran and won, holding the seat ever since. As a new judge, she thought she could make a positive difference. Her years on the bench had gradually convinced her that she couldn't.

The one remaining bright spot career-wise was her part-time teaching gig at the University of New Mexico's law school. She loved working with the students. Being around bright young people was invigorating and charged her mental batteries. She emphasized that the law should mete out justice, but with an underlying spirit of fairness. Maybe she was fooling herself. She wondered if she was just generating more lawyers like Espinoza's defense attorney, a former student she'd taught at UNM—lawyers whose twisted code of ethics was just about on a par as those held by their sleazy clients.

Despite her qualms about the future attorneys she was teaching, she valued her position at the university. Academia was so much simpler and safer than the real world. More than once, she'd considered quitting her judgeship in favor of a full-time teaching position, but she always pushed the thought away as being highly impractical.

Coming out of her reverie, she stared at the small statue of Lady Justice that occupied a spot on her credenza. Her dad had given it to her when she graduated law school. The famous figure of justice was depicted by a blindfolded lady holding a set of scales in balance. A quirky thought inspired her to fashion a dunce's cap from a piece of paper she tore from her notepad. Placing the dunce cap on the statue, she murmured, "Okay Justice, now you're not only blind, but you're also stupid as well."

She knew something had to give. Something had to change. She was becoming certain the time was right to finally act on the notions flitting around in her head. They could no longer be ignored.

She glanced at the clock on the wall, noting that Howard, her semi-significant-other for the last nineteen months, would arrive in front of the courthouse to pick her up in about fifteen minutes. She finished reviewing some paperwork for the next case on her docket, freshened up in the bathroom, put on a light jacket, and went down to wait for Howard outside on the courthouse steps. The evening breeze was only slightly chilly despite the fact that Albuquerque's elevation of over five thousand feet made it one of the country's highest cities, not far from being a close match in altitude to Denver. It could get pretty cold at night in the high desert, but for the time being, it was downright balmy and quite pleasant as spring drifted toward summer. The turmoil and frustration of the day gradually faded.

A bright red Corvette rumbled to a stop. The passenger side window went down, and Howard beamed at her from the driver's seat.

"Hey, sweet thing!" he shouted to her as she descended the steps. "You ready to rock 'n' roll?"

Despite her less-than-buoyant mood, she smiled at the man's lame attempt at jocularity. He was a nice enough guy, although a tad, perhaps a couple of tads, boring. But he possessed a playful side, oddly enough for a numbers person, and she liked that about him. In his mid-sixties, he was stable, financially secure, and handsome in a bookish kind of way. Howard was comfortably companionable, to the point that she could put up with his occasional boring rehashing of the daily goings on at his CPA firm—a change in the tax code, allowing a different depreciation schedule just didn't do it for her. The bottom line was she wanted more; she knew there would never be any real spark in her relationship with Howard.

She approached the car, went around to the passenger side, and got in. She put her purse next to her on the passenger seat and leaned over to give Howard a quick kiss on the lips.

"Hey, guy," she offered. "Boy, what a crappy day I had."

"Sorry to hear it," Howard said, putting the car in gear. "What serving of crap was on the menu today?"

"The usual, or it seems, usual more often these days. A case that should have been a slam dunk conviction went the other way. Idiotic jury found a scumbag rapist gangbanger innocent even though he was guilty as sin."

Howard pulled into traffic. Red taillights trailed in front of the vehicle. Stores, restaurants, and bars were lit up, pedestrians crowding the sidewalks. Downtown Albuquerque was living large on this warm spring evening.

"So," Romero said, glancing over at him, "how was your day?"

"Nothing to write home about. Same old, same old."

"Well, I guess that beats a crap show."

"Yeah, but not by a long shot. I wouldn't mind a small dose of excitement now and then. Might make the day go by faster," Howard said, laughing slightly.

Romero remained mostly silent for the rest of the drive, pondering what a "small dose of excitement" might entail for a guy like Howard. A miscalculated capital gain? Perhaps a paper jam in the copy machine? Mercifully, they arrived at the restaurant before she could fashion a retort.

"Well, here we are!" Howard said. "Don't know about you, but I'm starving!"

"Yeah, I could eat a horse," Romero said, grabbing her purse and getting out of the car.

"I don't think they serve that here," Howard said, taking her hand in his as they walked to the restaurant and went inside.

She registered the gesture, and she wondered whether the decision crystalizing in her mind would drive them apart. Money and status mattered deeply to Howard. How would he feel about her making a life-changing move at the age of fifty-five, at the height of her career as a judge? He enjoyed the prestige associated with dating a well-known judge. Frankly, she decided, as the hostess showed them to their table, she really didn't care all that much about how he felt. She cared for him, but this was about her. She was in the driver's seat, not him. Whatever she was deriving from their lukewarm, comfortable relationship wasn't sufficient to put her plans on hold.

They exchanged small talk, the usual chitchat about the weather, the current political mess in Washington, and the seemingly never-ending stream of craziness coming down from Santa Fe.

"Don't know when things will get better. I just know eventually they will," Howard said. "We can't stay in a recession forever. Everything comes in cycles."

Romero sipped her wine and nodded in agreement. "The upcoming elections this November ought to be interesting," she said, realizing that she'd just laid the groundwork for a perfect segue into what she wanted to discuss.

She took Howard's right hand in hers, leaned forward across the table, and said, "Howard, I've been thinking a lot about my career lately, and I think it's time for a change."

Romero saw the confusion flash across Howard's face as he crinkled his brow.

"What do you mean, make a change?"

"You know how unhappy I've been in my job lately. You know how disillusioned I am with the legal system. Like today. Like I told you. I presided over a rape and kidnapping case that should've been open-and-shut, but the creep got off. Jury let the jerk off when he should've been locked up for good."

"Uh-huh. Yeah, you've made it clear that you think the system is broken."

"It IS broken! And I don't see it getting better anytime soon. That's the problem. Nothing is changing, no matter what I do. No matter how hard I try to solve the nonsensical problems we face in our justice system, I get nowhere. I'm convinced now that a single person can't do jack to affect positive change."

Howard sighed and shook his head. "So, what are you getting at?"

"I've decided not to run for reelection this November. In fact, I'm thinking about resigning right away."

"You're kidding me, right?"

"No, I'm not."

"Yeah, you are! Bet you've gotten a sweet offer from Yates & Medoff or Hummer & Estrada. They've tried to bring you in as a partner several times."

"You'd lose that bet. No, let me explain. As you know, I've been volunteering at a Catholic clinic near Five Points for about a year. There's this priest, a Father Herb, who runs the place. I've told you about him."

"Yeah, you have," Howard said. "He's doing a lot to help many of the unwed young mothers in the neighborhood climb out of poverty, get their GEDs, that sort of thing, right?"

"That's right. I've been helping out, and it makes me feel good. I know I'm making a difference."

Howard took a sip of his wine and set the glass down, obviously slightly stunned.

"You're not kidding about leaving, are you?"

"No, I'm serious. I'm either going to resign or not run again, allowing me to spend more time at the clinic as well as more time teaching law students at UNM."

"You're crazy, Renee!" Howard said, raising his voice a bit. "Think of all the money you'll lose! Think of what you'll be giving up just to help poor Latina chicks in the barrio! That's just plain nuts."

Romero didn't like the way the conversation was going. Howard was really starting to annoy her. He focused only on his views, not hers; his needs and wants, not hers. His "poor Latina chicks in the barrio" remark really got under her skin. Given her background, how could he say something so insensitive?

She held up her left hand in front of his face. "You see this ring? It's a ring. It's not a dog tag. It's not a sign that you own me and can have a say over what I do or don't do. Not a chance in hell. I'd think you would have been more supportive of me and my needs. I'd have thought you'd want me to be happy regardless of financial considerations."

"I do want you to be happy. I just don't want you to make the biggest mistake of your life just because you feel guilty about not doing more to make the world a better place," Howard said.

"Well, you sure don't act like you care about my happiness."

"Let's not fight about this," Howard said.

"Little late for that," she said, fighting back her anger, tinged with sadness. He really didn't know her as well as she knew him.

They finished their meal in uneasy silence, broken only by occasional small talk that danced around the elephant in the room. The ride back to Romero's townhouse settled into glacial ice, which was fine with her. She didn't have anything more to say to him about her decision and was hurt that instead of offering his support he felt compelled to take on the role of an advisor, as if she weren't capable of chartering her own course.

As Howard pulled the corvette up in front of Romero's townhouse and came to a stop, he reached over and took her left hand in his.

"I'm sorry we fought," he said, sounding truly contrite. "I should've listened better. Given you the benefit of the doubt."

His words softened her emotions enough for her to squeeze his hand and say it was okay, even though it wasn't.

"If you think leaving the law is what will make you happy, then that's what I want for you."

"You're just saying that because I'm pissed off at how you reacted," Romero said, her anger bubbling up again. "You're all about money. That's all you ever seem to care about. Well, that's not for me. Not anymore. I want to die knowing I made a difference in the world. A positive difference. Right now, I'm making a negative difference. That's not going to be my legacy!"

"I get it, Renee," Howard said. He leaned over and kissed her on the cheek. "I'll wait here until you get safely inside."

Romero grabbed her purse, got out of the car, and stomped toward her door without saying goodnight. As she unlocked her front door, she couldn't help but feel a wave of relief over having finally told Howard about her plan. She had been dreading the confrontation, and now it was over. Howard's reaction solidified her conviction that it was time to make major life-changing decisions, personally and professionally. She thought about how happy Father Herb would be when she told him she'd be volunteering to work many more hours at the clinic than she had been able to commit to while she was performing her judicial duties. She opened the door, immediately being greeted by her energetic corgi, Georgie, who leapt at her as she stepped inside, barking his usual ecstatically happy greeting.

"Now you quiet down, Georgie! I'm home now! You'll get your gourmet dinner in a few minutes," she said, putting her purse on the table in the foyer and hanging her jacket in the closet.

Romero knelt down and scooped Georgie up into the crook of her right arm, kissing him smack on his plump black nose. Howard always hated it when she did that. He said it was really gross. And perhaps it was, but she didn't care. Her dog was the one life form on the planet she knew would never disappoint her. Why couldn't men be more like dogs—trustworthy, loving, and loyal to a fault?

"You're better than a man," she said, ruffling the short fur on his head. "Way, way, way better!"

"Okay, Georgie! What will it be for your dinner tonight? Your usual Friday night braised beef tips, or something special?"

3

Jim Viejo

AUGUST 2011

A WARM BREEZE BLEW IN OFF THE PACIFIC, FANNING THE dune grass into gentle motion. Gulls soared on the updrafts over the surf line. They wheeled and cawed in cacophonous abandon as Viejo walked alone on the dark, wet sand below the highwater mark, occasionally stopping to gaze vacantly out to sea, hoping to induce a relieving state of mental numbness. Serving the Medina death notice hit him hard. Each new notification reopened wounds on his scarred soul—wounds he doubted would ever heal, inflicted from the tragic losses of his wife and son. Sergeant Medina's notification could well be the proverbial straw that finally broke the camel's back.

You've got to decide, he thought. *Hell, you have decided. You're just afraid to pull the trigger.*

Viejo bent down and picked up a craggy piece of driftwood, bleached white from the sun. It almost looked like a cross. A sign, maybe? Vindication that his decision to retire and muster out immediately was the right one? For a moment, he thought it might be, but then his anger and cynicism about his current reality flared back. He was inclined to think God didn't really exist. How could so many bad things happen to so many good people, including himself?

He had wondered about that age-old question throughout his life as he observed the carnage people created. Personal tragedies had led him to wonder about it a lot more in recent months. Was he good at his core, or as evil, or perhaps more evil than most people? Inherently bad, or inherently good? Maybe he was just not in touch with whatever goodness he possessed. Viejo wasn't sure. He wasn't sure about much anymore. The simple, childlike faith his parents had taught him had withered in the face of his personal tragedies.

He threw the stick into the rolling surf's breaking white crests. Newly arriving waves caught it and tossed it about until the undertow dragged it toward another distant beach, perhaps to provide a divinely sent sign to some stranger more willing to take note. Camp Pendleton's beauty offered a source of private solace whenever he availed himself of the opportunity to partake of quiet moments away from the camp's constant insane collage of activity. Betti had enjoyed their hikes together, exploring the natural wonders of the base. He would have given anything to be enjoying this beautiful evening with her.

He heard the sound of an engine over the ocean gusts. He turned around and saw a Jeep coming toward him at speed, kicking up clouds of fine white sand in its wake. The Jeep loomed ever closer as Viejo stood stock still, arms akimbo, watching the dark green shape grow more distinct. He wondered just how far he'd walked. Time stopped when he was on the beach, lost in his own head. Had he inadvertently strayed into a restricted area?

The sound of the engine grew louder as the Jeep approached, drawing close enough for Viejo to see who was driving.

Ross, of course, he thought, smiling slightly at the sight of his close friend.

The Jeep pulled up to him, and General Marks stopped, shooting Viejo a big, toothy, white smile.

"Well, what brings you way out here?" Marks asked, stepping out of the Jeep.

General Marks hadn't changed all that much in the more than three decades of their friendship. He stood above six feet tall, maybe weighed ten pounds more than when they'd first met. His dark black skin glistened with a slight sheen of sweat. Marks was wearing baggy shorts and a Marine T-shirt. His large brown eyes reflected the extent of his concern for Viejo, something not lost on Viejo as he observed his friend striding toward him on the deserted beach.

"Hey," Viejo said, sounding as dejected as he felt.

"Hey, yourself," Marks said.

Marks stepped forward and gave Viejo a man hug. Viejo returned it.

"Seriously," Marks said, "what are you doing way out here? You must've walked for miles."

"Looks like I did. Wasn't paying much attention to time, I guess."

"Just out for some fresh air, I suppose."

"Something like that."

Marks leaned against the side of the Jeep. He unwrapped a thick cigar, cut the tip off, and used a flame-thrower lighter to light up. He took a long drag and blew a huge cloud of blue smoke, making him look a little like a thin black dragon.

"Want one?" he asked Viejo. "I brought another one, just in case."

Viejo considered the offer. Actually, a good smoke sounded pretty enticing at the moment.

"Sure," he said.

Marks pulled another cigar from his shorts pocket and handed it to Viejo.

"Enjoy," Marks said.

Viejo accepted the cigar, and Marks helped him light it. He leaned against the Jeep next to his friend as they both smoked in companionable silence.

"I also brought something else," Marks said.

He reached into the back seat and took out a full bottle of Johnnie Walker Blue Label.

"I've been saving this for a special occasion," Marks said.

Viejo grinned. He hadn't seen Marks yank out the precious stuff in years. What was all the fuss was about? Did Marks somehow know that he'd finally made up his mind to ditch his career in the Marine Corps? Marks and he had always shared an almost supernatural cognitive connection, almost like a sixth sense.

"You've pulled out all the stops, man," Viejo said, smiling broadly as Marks set the bottle on the hood and produced two highball glasses from the back seat. He handed one to Viejo. "What'd that bottle cost you? A second mortgage?"

Both men laughed.

"I figured you could use some company," Marks said, pouring a generous amount of scotch into each glass.

His friend's strategy was having the designed effect. He picked up the glass, took a soothing sip, and dragged deeply on the cigar. Great booze, a super smoke, and a lifelong friend. Not a bad way to watch the sun go down . . . what life was all about at its best—at least about the best one could expect as a member of our poorly evolved species. For a moment, Viejo thought he might miss his career in the Marines. After all, it represented the essence of his identity, who he was as a man, as an individual, and his spot on the great mandala.

"Thanks, Ross," Viejo said. He held up his glass for a toast. "Cheers," he said and clinked glasses with Marks.

"Cheers, my friend," Marks said.

Viejo looked out to sea, not wanting to disturb the tranquility of the moment, but then he decided to take the plunge.

"I think I should tell you something," Viejo said.

"What?" Marks asked, raising his left eyebrow like he always did when he wanted to know the answer to a question.

"I want out," Viejo said. "I can't take it anymore . . . being in the Marines. I'm burned out. Used up. Washed up."

Marks dragged on his cigar and said, "I thought this was coming. Wasn't hard to see. Was pretty sure you were going to share the news. You sure about this?"

Viejo nodded. "Yeah, I'm sure. Hell, I've been in for thirty-six years. As you well know, the top brass passed me over for promotion again. The writing is on the wall. They want me out. I've gone as far as I can go, maybe further than I should have. What's that old saw about people rising to the level of their incompetence?"

"To be frank, that's accurate. You've reached the end of the line, I'm afraid. The temper flare-ups, the moodiness, and your general lack of gumption in recent years have not gone unnoticed. You know I've spoken to you about this before, and—"

"Yeah, yeah, yeah. I know. That's why I've decided to do everyone a favor and bug out."

"It's a shame things had to turn out this way," Marks said. "I, for one, am going to miss the hell out of having you around here. Hell, a lot of us will miss you."

"Being missed by a few people isn't much of a legacy," Viejo said, laughing for the second time that day. "I had a wart cut off my butt a few years ago, and for a while, I missed it . . . not a bad analogy if you think about it . . . I've become sort of like a wart, a useless body part serving no discernible purpose."

They slipped into the comfortable silence typical of old friends, sipping their scotch, dragging on the cigars, and gazing admiringly at the broad blue Pacific stretched out before them in a seemingly limitless expanse.

"So, what are your plans, then?" Marks asked.

"I'm heading to Albuquerque to be with my family. I haven't had much of a family life since Betti died. What with Michael being KIA, we've all sort of drifted apart, or at least I have. As a father and a grandfather, I've been AWOL. I've been lost in my own self-created hell, and I think the only way out of it is to make a huge change in my life. A change for the better. Reconnecting with my family seems like a helluva good start. I am extremely lucky that Mary Jane and her family are welcoming me back into the fold. She's even offered to let me move in with them for as long as I want. I am going to do my best not to bring my dark side with me, at least not so the family will ever see it. They are only going to see encouragement and love, none of the bad stuff. "

Marks slapped him on the back. "Now you're talking! Sounds like a great plan, Jim. You're tough enough to make this work. I've been wondering when you were going to get up off your sorry ass and make some assertive changes in your life. This camp is just giving you a place to hide. You can't stay mired in grief forever. Hell, man! You've got your whole life ahead of you."

"Rah, rah, sis boom bah!"

"Very funny," Marks said.

"You're my very own cheerleading squad."

"Sometimes, a guy needs one."

It felt good to finally tell his friend about his decision. Verbalizing it to another person somehow made it seem more real, more final—like it was already happening.

"Any idea what you'll do out there? You don't really have to work," Marks said. "You've got the VA benefits in addition to your pension. Financially, you're set as long as you don't blow the bank on something really stupid."

"I dunno, Ross," Viejo said. "Haven't given it much thought. I know I can't just sit around. I have to be busy. But at least it won't be delivering death notices to wives and mothers."

"I know," Marks said. "That has to be the worst duty in the military."

"Well, not for me anymore. I'm done. *Fini.* Kaput!"

"Just don't waste any time looking in your rearview mirror. Concentrate on what's ahead of you."

"I hope I can pull this off without dragging anyone down with me."

"Hope doesn't help if it doesn't lead to action," Marks said. "Betti would want you to find happiness again, and to do that, you have to want to be happy. She would want that for you."

Viejo felt another surge of raw grief, all too familiar in recent years. "Yeah, I know. You're right, of course. She wouldn't want me wallowing around in my own living hell. I know that. But sometimes it's hard to crawl out of the hole, you know? Sometimes, it just seems impossible."

"I've always had faith in you, Jim," Marks said. "And so did Betti. She still does as she watches over you from heaven. Five years ago, you were the strongest guy I ever met. You need to find that guy again."

"You know, there are times when I think she's in the room with me. I talk to her sometimes. Actually, I talk to her a lot."

"That's entirely normal."

"The feeling that she's there is so real, though."

"Don't fight it. Take comfort in it. You never know. There are many things in this life we can't explain. I've always believed there was a higher being, God, if you will, or something else we can't even imagine is out there somewhere. So, if you feel Betti visits you to give you comfort, wrap your arms around it. Never look a gift horse in the mouth."

4

Betti

MY SPIRIT REMAINS EARTHBOUND. I LINGER INSIDE THE music box I had Viejo place my ashes in. I won't make my final ascension to my soul's rightful place until I know Jim will be alright. This is my decision. God has allowed it as a concession for the deep love Jim and I shared while I was alive. I remain spiritually near the man I still love with every bit of my essence. I can't talk to him, but I know he senses my presence.

When I was on my deathbed, the cancer having almost won its war against me, I held Viejo's hand in mine as he sat at my bedside and made him promise to move on with his life after my death. I made him promise to find love with another woman and to not live in darkness and loneliness. It was a moment I'll always remember—the pain in his eyes, the unspeakable depths of his sadness. I feel it to this very day. More than anything, I want him to heal.

When a true love is lost to the natural cycle of death, it's even more painful than the suffering that occurs after a marriage ends in divorce. In either case, the gaping hole left behind is typically never really filled without a concerted effort on the part of the griever. The person must make a conscious effort to face the grief, acknowledge it, and defeat it. Jim hasn't done that. He's still running away from his emotions and pain. Has to draw upon his inner toughness, and fight. Stand up to his grief, and overcome it, before he can successfully move on toward happiness. His best first step is to stop popping valium and drinking too much alcohol in his futile effort to flee from himself. It frustrates me that I'm restricted to the role of an observer, that I'm powerless to communicate directly with him.

I am watching as he finishes the last of his packing up at base housing. I'm glad he's retiring from the Marines and that he's moving to Albuquerque to be near Mary Jane and the grandkids. The job has been eating him alive for years. He's finally reached the breaking point. I hate to think what might have happened if he stayed in the Corps.

He's just left the apartment with the last of his boxes. He's traveling light after getting rid of most of his belongings. Starting out nice and fresh. That's a good thing, in my view. The door to the apartment swings open and Jim approaches my music box. He picks it up, winds the music box, and the melody of our favorite song plays *Somewhere Over the Rainbow*, Judy Garland's signature song from the 1939 movie *Wizard of Oz*. The song symbolized the importance of treasuring what was important in our lives. Playing it gives Jim comfort. It continues to comfort me as well.

He's smiling and crying at the same time. Grief is always a messy mix. He's been wallowing in it for far too long.

"Betti," he says, "it's so hard living without you and Michael in my life. I feel empty inside. I know to honor your memory I must keep going. You would be disappointed in me for being the way I am now. I promise I will do everything within my power to contain this for the sake of our family and not let it show on the outside. Fake it 'til I make it . . . don't know if I ever will 'make it,' but I'm not going to spend the rest of my life as the poster child for depression."

I wish I could answer him. I'm simply a presence who can't be seen, only felt, if he's open to sensing me. I desperately want Jim to find happiness. I pray he will honor his last promise to me.

The song ends. Viejo clasps my music box with both hands on either side and lifts it up from the kitchen counter, holding it close to his face. I see the deep sadness in his eyes and I radiate all the love I can generate.

"Come on, Betti," he says, "it's time to go."

He carries my music box out to his black SUV, opens the front passenger side door, and secures my music box with the seatbelt.

"Don't want you to end up all over the floorboards, honey," he says. "I'm not ready to scatter you yet. Someday, maybe, but not today."

Viejo closes the front door, goes around to the driver's side, gets in, and fires up the engine. He stares at the apartment complex. I can feel his mix of emotions. He's excited and yet sad at the same time. As he pulls away and drives off base to the interstate, I share in his positive hope for the future. What happens next is anybody's guess, though I am certain God is in charge. I have faith in Him. I know everything is going to be okay. With God, all things are possible.

5

Renee Romero

PRESENT TIMES

RENEE TURNED OFF SOUTH BROADWAY, NAVIGATING through small side streets on her way to Holy Mother Outreach Clinic. No matter how many times she came this way, it always saddened her to see what had become of the neighborhood. Although never a high-end, or even a middle-class area, it had been a safe place to live. Small, neatly kept houses, well-maintained locally owned businesses, and attractive parks had evidenced pride among the residents. Neighborhood kids were safe to ride their bikes, walk to school, and play in the parks without any fear of danger. Everybody knew everybody. If you got into any minor mischief, your parents would likely have heard about it before you got home.

It was hardly recognizable now. Most of the old neighbors had either died or moved away. Urban decay had taken its toll. The residential areas were mostly homes in various stages of disrepair or trashy vacant lots. The thriving small shops of her youth were now vacant and boarded up. Graffiti was everywhere, primarily gang territorial signs.

She pulled up in front of the clinic and parked. The old building had originally been built to serve as a small community Catholic Church. It had become vacant years ago after the Diocese decided to combine several of the smaller churches into a larger church located in a safer neighborhood. Father Herb had inherited some family money, which he used to purchase the property and remodel it for use as the clinic.

Romero sat in the car with her eyes shut, preparing for her upcoming meeting with Father Herb. The thump-thump-thump of a heavy bass blaring from the stereo of an old black Chevy cruising toward her broke her concentration. The car was packed with stereotypical gangbangers, obviously with nothing better to do than ride around looking for trouble while making their presence known in the neighborhood.

As she exited her forest-green Lexus, she noticed along the usual assortment of trash blowing around on the gentle spring breeze, the distinct fragrance of weed emanating from a group of teenagers across the street. They were poster children for inner-city societal problems. Young men with no hope for the future and a tremendous need to fit in somewhere, anywhere. Sadly, their natural human need to belong usually meant ending up in a gang with criminals for role models.

Romero gazed up at the sign above the door. Below the name of the clinic was the slogan, "Seize tomorrow by preparing today," and the phrase *"Esperanza por el futuro,"* Spanish for "Hope for the future." These words were intended to inspire hope in the lives of those the clinic served.

Father Herb's mission was simple, aptly defined by the phrases on the door. He wanted to create opportunities and new directions for the neighborhood youth, especially teenage girls who were all too often lured into pregnancy by guys who professed love, but were only interested in proving their virility by impregnating as many "baby mamas" as possible. The girls were easy prey, as many had no traditional home lives, being raised by mothers who had fallen into the same trap. Having a baby to care for, and no marketable skills or parental support, many of the girls dropped out of school and drifted into prostitution, with their "baby daddies" serving as pimps to generate money, used selfishly for themselves, rarely to support the girls and their babies. The clinic provided day care services, while helping the girls to either complete high school or obtain their GED, and also offered job training along with placement services. Herb was seeing gradual change, as girls in the neighborhood recognized the clinic as their only way out of the trap.

"Yo, judge! You back here again?" one of the bangers called to her, a big muscular guy she recognized as one of the leaders, a bad dude named Roque Sanchez. "You sure you wanna park that fancy ride here? Somethin' bad might happen to it."

Romero was used to being harassed whenever she parked at the clinic. She didn't worry too much about the local heavies because she knew they realized she was a district court judge. Chances were good that a gang member would end up in her courtroom one day, and most of them were at least bright enough to recognize the consequences. The last thing they wanted was to piss off a person who might hold their liberty in her hands.

She glared at Roque, knowing she shouldn't rise to the bait, but doing so anyway, she shouted, "Yeah, go ahead and mess with my car. You'd look good in prison stripes! Bet some of those big old muscle-bound prisoners might think you're pretty cute if you catch my drift."

Roque laughed and slapped his thighs with both hands. "Woo-hoo! She's one sassy little bowl of salsa, no?" he said, turning to his compadres.

"And hot too!" another banger said. "Smokin' hot! *Muy caliente!*"

Romero knew she was hot. Her slim, curvaceous figure belied the fact that she was fifty-five. Hispanic father and Irish mother's genes provided her with the sultry looks of a Latina with shoulder-length auburn hair and Irish emerald-green eyes. That didn't mean she wanted attention from any of them.

"Keep an eye on the car for me, Mr. Sanchez!" Romero said, knowing she was taunting him.

"Maybe I'll do more than that!"

"Don't forget," she said, her voice stern, "I know where you live now, and I also know where you'll be living after I have you arrested."

"Don't be so sure about that."

She hit the lock button on her key fob and walked to the entrance of the building, feeling the banger's leering eyes on her back. She felt mild fear, but mostly disgust. Guys like Roque were the core of the city's problem when it came to dysfunctional neighborhoods and families. Poverty and crime thrived in the gang-enforced environment; aided unwittingly by local politicians, who wrote off low-income ethnic neighborhoods as unredeemable. It was incumbent upon the gangs to keep the chaos going at all costs. Where chaos reigned, law and order became tenuous, keeping the gang culture alive and thriving.

Romero strolled into the clinic and smiled broadly at Jessica Marquez, Father Herb's able assistant, who was seated at the front desk. Jessica always sported an infectious smile, always radiating enthusiasm and genuine concern for coworkers and clients. She'd first come to the clinic several years earlier as a teenage mom, struggling with the challenge of raising a mentally challenged baby who needed a lot of special care. Her family was nonexistent, and, of course, the father didn't give a rat's ass about the mother or his child. She excelled in her studies at the clinic. After she graduated, Father Herb had wisely hired her full time at the clinic. She built a decent, wholesome life under Father Herb's guidance. He often used her as an example to the young girls as to what they could become.

"Hey, Jessie," Romero said as she came in. "What's shakin'?"

Jessie laughed and returned Romero's smile. "Be a lot of my body parts if I don't lay off the donuts . . . just the same old stuff, Renee. Can't complain. In fact, everything's peachy."

"Glad to hear it," Romero said. "Father Herb's expecting me."

"Yes, he told me you were coming in for a special meeting. Mind telling me what this is all about?"

Romero leaned across Jessie's desk and whispered in her ear. "Father Herb should probably be the first to know, but since you asked, I've resigned my judgeship. I'm going to seriously up my volunteer hours at the clinic."

"That's wonderful!" Jessie said, leaning back in her seat. "We need all the help we can get. But why did you ditch your career? You're not old enough to retire."

"Lots of reasons I don't want to get into now, but maybe we can get together for a cup of coffee and one of your nemesis donuts. I can fill you in."

"That'd be fabulous," Jessie said. "Except for the part where I lose another battle with the donut devil. Go on through. Don't want to keep Father Herb waiting."

Romero walked briskly down the hall. On either side were classrooms filled with kids of all ages, but mostly teenage girls. Funded by private charities and corporations, a mixture of salaried and volunteer teachers presided over classrooms, teaching basic math and reading, while other classrooms served as computer stations or study halls. She passed the medical office, feeling blessed that she had been able to provide most of the funding for the clinic's medical services. A full-time nurse practitioner provided basic healthcare, including the issuance of contraceptives. The birth control help was frowned upon by many in the Diocese. Father Herb didn't care. He insisted that preventing pregnancies in the first place made the most sense in his effort to deal with the problems the girls faced in their everyday lives. The nurse also taught sex education, constantly warning the girls about the dangers of getting pregnant at an early age with no familial support to fall back on. A smile flashed across her face, as she had a brief memory of her dad's rhythm and bingo joke.

Herb's modest office was at the end of the long hall. The door was wide open, and she saw Herb sitting behind his desk with a big grin on his face. He was becoming elderly, but camouflaging it well. Mexican descent, his family legally migrated to the United States a generation ago and eventually settled in San Antonio. He stood about five-eight, had salt-and-pepper, mostly salt hair, and thick eyebrows. His weathered skin bore evidence from decades working in the fields before entering the priesthood. He was clean shaven and muscular in build. Judging by the way he carried himself, one would think that in his youth, he could have gone toe-to-toe with the toughest of gangbangers without giving an inch. She genuinely liked Father Herb. There was a spiritual quality about him that touched her heart in a way she didn't completely understand.

"Well, there she is!" Herb said, standing up from behind his desk. "My nonjudgmental judge!"

He came around his desk and gave Romero a gentle hug, patting her three times on the shoulder.

"Come, sit down. Take a load off."

Romero smiled back at him as she sat down in one of the chairs in front of Herb's desk. She crossed her legs and leaned back in a comfortable position.

"*Como estas*, Father Herb?" she asked, resting both hands on the arms of the chair.

"*Muy bien*! Not bad at all, at least in the big scene of things."

"Wait a minute here . . . you are always telling me not to sweat the small stuff, and that in reality, it's all small stuff. Did you have a recent epiphany?" she chided.

Holding his hands up in mock surrender. "Okay, you got me this time. We'll resolve this paradox over a glass of wine sometime."

"I've got something exciting to tell you, Father Herb."

"And what might that be?"

He looked genuinely curious, but she also got the sense that he already knew what she was going to say. She didn't know how she knew that he knew . . . probably related to that mysterious spiritual quality she couldn't quite define.

"I've resigned my judgeship! I'll have to work through my current caseload, but I should be done in a couple of months."

Father Herb raised both eyebrows. "You don't say! Why? What happened? What made you jump ship at such a young age?"

Romero expected this line of questioning. "I guess fifty-five seems young to you. I bet you've got socks that old!" Turning serious, she offered, "You're a big part of this. You helped me to understand why I've been so unhappy in recent years. I know my dirtbag ex-husband contributed to my unhappiness. Hell, uh, . . . sorry, heck, he made me downright miserable, and that was before I found out he was cheating on me. I thought I could just bury myself in the job and gain a sense of peace and satisfaction. But, no, you've shown me it's better to give back than to be in the punishment business, and that's pretty much all I've been doing as a judge. In view of how many guilty perps get off, I'm not even very effective in the punishment business."

"Judges are supposed to be in the punishment business," Father Herb said, "but I can see how you could become disillusioned with the justice system. It certainly isn't perfect."

Romero sighed and said, "No, it certainly isn't. In fact, it's broken. Dysfunctional. Unfair. Especially for the disadvantaged. I'm sick of it, which is why I am quitting. I'd like to increase my volunteer hours here. I know I've been helping you with legal matters, but I can do a lot more than that—like help with fundraising, especially corporate donations. I can expand my tutoring sessions for kids studying for their GEDs; make a positive difference in someone's life for a change. Be that ounce of prevention instead of a pound of cure."

Rubbing his hands together, Father Herb beamed at Romero. "Why am I not surprised that you're doing this? I sorta had a feeling you were about to make a big move. You could say a little bird told me."

"Uh-huh," Romero said, fiddling with her purse. "A little bird, you say?"

"Something like that . . . definitely had wings. I get messages from lots of places, as you so well know. For example, I know Howard disagreed with your decision."

His remark puzzled her. How could he know how Howard reacted to her news? Dismissing that thought, she said, "I saw Roque Sanchez again out on the corner in front of the clinic. He hassled me on the way in."

Father Herb's face went deadly serious. He steepled his fingers and leaned forward over his desk, fixing Romero with a stare that was rather unpriestly.

"You say Roque bothered you? What did he do?"

"Nothing really," she said. "He's just being his usual intimidating self. I do worry that he and his crew are making it tough for the kids and our staff when they come in for class or daycare. They practically have to walk a gauntlet to get to the front door."

"That's what he wants . . . especially the girls. Scare them away, so they stay under his thumb. If they're here learning to be independent, they won't be out selling themselves for him. We could eventually be putting him and his like out of business in this neighborhood."

Father Herb stood up from his desk and went to the window overlooking the adjacent vacant lot. He folded his hands behind his back as he paced back and forth.

"Roque and his crew have been getting much more aggressive lately, and I've talked to Detective Fermin Padilla with the city police department. He says there's a big push from the cartels down in Mexico to boost revenue in Albuquerque from drug sales and prostitution. At least that's the word on the street."

"What does that mean for the clinic?"

Father Herb turned away from the window and sat down again. "It means that doing business as usual may become more difficult," Father Herb said. "Frankly, I'm concerned. Things are going well at the moment, but that could change in a heartbeat."

"Well, I guess we'll just have to keep doing the best we can for the girls and, come what may."

"Exactly," Father Herb said. "Come what may. But I can tell you a little bird told me that help is on the way."

"What do you mean?" Romero asked.

Father Herb grinned, showing his perfect white teeth. "Let me just say that God works in mysterious ways!"

6

Jim Veijo

PRESENT TIMES

RECENTLY RETIRED COLONEL JAMES VIEJO DROVE JUST over the speed limit, heading east on I-40 through Arizona on his way to Albuquerque. He'd driven steadily for hours, eager to reach his daughter's home and call it a day. He was thankful that she'd invited him to stay with Peyton and the kids for as long as he wanted. They seemed anxious to reconnect with him and were thrilled he was moving to the city to be closer to them. Peyton had proven to be a terrific husband and father. He couldn't wait to see them. The pain and despair he felt so intensely in recent months diminished with every passing mile. He had made the right decision. Why had he taken so long? Probably, the valium had something to do with that. He was determined to contain his inner turmoil. As far as they would know, he was back to his old self, the fun-loving father and grandfather they remembered from years ago.

Viejo looked forward to starting over. He had no idea what he would do to fill the empty hours of each day or what would give his life purpose. It wasn't enough to simply survive. He would need a reason to get up every morning. His father had told him long ago that a life without purpose was no life at all, just marking time until your funeral. He recalled reading a study about the longevity of retired military officers . . . the ones who went on to new careers generally far outlived those who didn't. The Marine Corps had given him purpose for over three decades. Now that he was out, he could no longer ground his identity in the military. He was excited about his decision, but also worried that he might drift into an even deeper depression if he was unable to find something worthwhile to do. He couldn't afford to let that happen for his family's sake, as well as his own.

Thoughts of Betti flitted through his mind as he drove on in silence. He usually listened to classic rock stations while driving, but today, he was using the quiet time for some reflection. He pictured his wife, a petite blonde with bright blue eyes and an athletic figure. She was a graduate of the University of New Mexico's sociology program and took a job offer to work for the City of Albuquerque's Child Protective Services after graduating cum laude in 1968.

After his first tour of duty in Vietnam ended in 1970, he returned on leave to his small hometown in Southern New Mexico to lick his physical and emotional wounds. He was mentally tough, darn hard to break, but what he experienced in the jungles of Nam had taken its toll. Near the end of his leave time, he'd driven up to Albuquerque to visit with Ross Marks, who had made a seemingly miraculous recovery from his wounds and was about to enter the Marine Officer Training Program. Observing Ross in combat, Viejo recognized outstanding bravery and leadership qualities. He had encouraged Ross to become an officer and see how far he could go in the Corps., telling Ross, "The Marines don't care about skin color. It's guts and ability that matter, and you have both of those in spades . . . no racial pun intended."

Viejo was deploying again at the end of his leave time. He'd attended the state university on an ROTC scholarship, where he graduated with a degree in engineering in the spring of 1967. He was required to go on active duty in return for the scholarship he'd received. Without it, he'd never have been able to afford the tuition.

While Viejo was in Albuquerque, Marks threw a big party to celebrate his acceptance at OCS. As fate would have it, Betti, a friend of Ross's girlfriend, was at the party. When Viejo laid eyes on Betti, it was love at first sight, like a scene from some sappy romantic movie. He smiled, reliving the moment in his head as he continued driving toward the city.

He recalled locking eyes with her across the crowded room and thought he detected a little encouragement. He pushed through the crowd and stood in front of Betti, smiling down at her. She stood barely over five feet, clad in tight jeans and a Doors T-shirt. He noticed she wore very little makeup. She didn't need to, in his opinion. Her soft white skin was blemish-free. Her full lips turned up in a warm, inviting smile.

"Hi, I'm Viejo," he shouted over the music. "Good friend of Ross's."

Betti introduced herself.

"So, how do you know Ross?" Viejo asked.

"Don't know him all that well. He's been dating my best friend, Sheila, for a couple of months. Seems like a really great guy. War hero. Wants to be an officer. Perfect gentleman around Sheila. The kind of guy who's hard to find nowadays. That's about all I know about him. How do you know Ross?"

"We served together in Nam," Viejo said. He thought it best to play it humble and not mention anything about his saving Ross's life. She didn't seem like a girl who would be impressed by a guy who tooted his own horn.

Tired of having to shout over the music, he asked if she wanted to step outside for some fresh air. She did. The connection between them was immediate and powerful. They talked for hours, not realizing how much time was passing, until Ross came out and told them the party had ended and all the other guests had gone. Viejo asked her if she would have dinner with him the next evening. She agreed and suggested they meet at a popular café in the Old Town area.

* * *

They began dating, and after somewhat of a whirlwind romance, they got married less than a year later in a simple ceremony on the beach. Although they didn't get much of a honeymoon, Viejo managed to get leave time for R&R on Oahu. Five days later, Viejo was on his way back to Vietnam. The last few months of his tour passed excruciatingly slowly as they waited to be together again.

A sudden horn blast from the car behind him shook him out of his daydream. He had been dawdling along in the passing lane, apparently infuriating the driver behind him. Viejo pulled over to the righthand lane to allow the guy to pass, giving him a sheepish grin as he sped by. Unappeased by Viejo's act of penance, the guy shot him the finger, honked again, and sped on his way.

As he rounded the next curve, Viejo approached an old Winnebago pulled over on the side of the highway, its left rear tire flat. An old couple stood looking at the flat. The man held a jack in his hands. Viejo rubbernecked on the way by, but he kept going, focused solely on getting to Mary Jane's house in time for dinner. As he drove on, he felt guilty about not stopping to help. It was completely out of his character not to stop and offer assistance.

Oddly, he got a strong sense of Betti's presence. That had been happening more often of late, and this time, he could practically feel her on his skin, in the air, everywhere. For a split second, he swore he smelled her favorite perfume.

"Betti?" he asked. "You there?"

Of course, he didn't expect her to answer him.

"I know, I know. I should've stopped to help them," he said, heaving a deep sigh.

Cursing his conscience, he made a U-turn at the next crossover and drove the couple of miles back to the Winnebago. As he pulled up and parked, he noticed an apparent good Samaritan who had stopped to help. He also noticed the Harley the guy had been riding. A brilliant white monster hog that looked almost brand-new. The polished chrome glistened in the high desert sun, giving the bike an almost surreal appearance.

"Looks like you guys could use a hand," Viejo said as he walked over to where the two men were standing, their eyes shifting back and forth between the flat and the spare tire attached to the rear of the RV.

"Yeah, we sure could," the old man said.

"Glad you turned around," the biker said.

The comment puzzled Viejo, but he dismissed it.

"Those tires are super heavy," the biker observed.

"Yeah, they look like they weigh a ton," Viejo said.

"They do," the old man said. "I wouldn't have been able to change the tire all by myself. Triple-A said it would take over two hours for them to get someone here."

"Well, don't worry about that now. We're here to help. You'll be back on the road in no time," the biker replied. "Okay, then. Let's get to work!"

Viejo helped the biker jack up the RV and remove the flat, largely in silence as they both focused on the task at hand. A short time later, the tire was changed. The couple was elated and highly grateful. They offered to pay them for their efforts, but both men refused.

"Just pay it forward," the biker suggested. "Next time someone needs help, step up and help if you can."

"Oh, we will," the man's wife said with a broad smile. "You can count on that."

"I know I can," the biker said. "I know all about you two. You're good people through and through. You should be proud of the wholesome lives you've led, the kindness you've shown to others in the past. All that good stuff."

Viejo saw the puzzlement on their faces. He thought this biker guy was a really weird duck. How could he know these things about the couple? Or the fact that he had initially passed by the old couple before his conscience kicked in. It just didn't make any sense. It stoked his curiosity. The old couple got in the Winnebago, waited for a break in traffic, and merged back onto the highway. After watching the old Winnebago disappear into the distance, Viejo turned to face the guy.

"How did you know I came back to help?" Viejo asked.

"I know everything about you, Colonel."

"How did you know I was a colonel?" Viejo asked, feeling more surprised every second.

" I know lots of things. You've been popping valium and drinking too much. You've been so depressed you think you can't keep going. Our meeting isn't accidental."

Confused and suspicious, Viejo wasn't sure what to make of this peculiar man. He didn't get a sense that he was being toyed with or that he was some kind of con artist. The opposite, in fact. But how could a complete stranger know he was abusing valium? And the other stuff? How could he know that?

"I don't know what you're playing at, but I can tell you I don't like it. It's creepy how you know things like that about me. How could you know what drugs I take? That I've been depressed?"

He shot Viejo a serious look, an obvious forerunner of an important message.

"There are things in life you can't possibly understand, Jim. You've got to take it on faith. If I told you God shared a vision of you with me, would you believe it?"

"No."

"I figured as much. But that's okay. You'll come around eventually. Like, for instance, you just passed your first big test."

Viejo was becoming agitated. It was all so confusing and weird.

"What big test?"

"The big guy upstairs and I devised the test with the Winnebago to see if you were ready to move ahead with the next phase. If you had just kept going, it would have shown us you weren't ready for your mission."

"What the hell are you talking about? What mission?"

"You're not ready for the answer. It will be clear soon enough. There will be signs."

"Signs? What signs? The only sign I see right now is the one over there that tells me how far it is to the next exit."

"For the time being, it's the same non-answer as before. The process doesn't work that way. Signs don't work if you can see them coming. God doesn't telegraph his pitches."

"God's a pitcher? Seems like all I've been getting from him are bean balls, and I wasn't provided with a batting helmet."

"I know you don't believe me," he said as he mounted the Harley.

"About as much as I believe in the Easter Bunny."

"Thanks for helping out!" He waved and blasted off in a spray of gravel, leaving Viejo staring after him in stunned silence.

"That was too weird!" Viejo said aloud as he got back into his SUV. "Maybe there are some side effects to my drugs I'm not aware of . . .

hallucinations? Daydreams? Did this really just happen? I'm only a few hours away from the alien incidents in Roswell; maybe I just had a close encounter of the third kind?"

The sun was almost down by the time Viejo turned onto Mary Jane's street in Northeast Heights, a nice middle-class section of the city. He pulled into the driveway and shut down the engine just as his daughter and her family poured out of the front door, shouting greetings as they surrounded and hugged him. Tootie, the family's little dachshund, circled the group, yapping excitedly.

"I'm so glad you're here, Dad!" Mary Jane gushed.

She looked happy and healthy, the streaks of gray in her hair showing the passage of the years. It seemed to Viejo like only yesterday she'd been a baby thrashing about in her crib.

"Glad to be here."

"How was the trip?" Peyton asked. "Smooth sailing, I hope."

"Yeah, it was fine. Not too much traffic on I-40. Mostly uneventful." Viejo thought the better of mentioning the Winnebago incident. They might decide that he needed to be living in a psyche ward, instead of with them.

"Come on, kids," Mary Jane said, "let's get this car unloaded before dinner!"

Mary Jane clapped her hands together as if to signal the start of a race. Meghan, his twenty-year-old granddaughter, and the thirteen-year-old twins, Harrison and Wesley, eager to help, grabbed boxes and suitcases and began energetically taking his belongings to the back bedroom, a spacious guest accommodation furnished with an eye toward subtle luxury.

Mary Jane helped him unpack while the kids continued unloading the car.

"How do you feel now that you're done with the Marines?" she asked. "Retiring must've been a big decision for you."

"It wasn't, really. My career was pretty much over at this point. My heart just wasn't into the assignments I was getting. Didn't use to think of it that way. Now I see myself as part of the problem, part of spreading misery around. If every politician promoting war would have to perform death notice duty, it might change the way they think."

"Well, that's profound, Dad," Mary Jane said, hanging some shirts up in the closet. "I'll iron these for you later."

"I've been thinking a lot about life these days. Your mom and Michael."

"Kinda figured that," she said.

They worked in silence for a few moments.

"It's striking how much you look like your mom," Viejo said. "I've always thought the resemblance was uncanny, almost like you were cloned."

Mary Jane laughed. "You always said that, Dad."

"When the shoe fits."

Just then, Meghan hurried in, carrying the music box filled with Betti's ashes. Her right foot snagged on the carpet and she almost tripped.

"Oh, no!" she cried, staggering to keep her balance.

Anger briefly flared up in Viejo, triggered by his instinct to protect Betti, even in ash form. He managed to conceal the reaction and smiled at his granddaughter, warning her that it wouldn't be good if she had to vacuum her grandma's ashes up.

"Sorry, Grandma wouldn't be happy ending up in a vacuum cleaner!" Meghan apologized.

"Yeah, knowing her, she would probably say it sucked," Viejo offered, defusing the situation with an attempt at humor.

He saw simultaneous eye rolls from his daughter and granddaughter.

"I had almost forgotten how bad your jokes are, Dad," Mary Jane said, giggling.

The twins came in with the last of the boxes.

"What's going on?"

"Oh, your sister nearly took a spill, that's all. No big deal since it didn't happen," Viejo said.

"Okay, I would have found the whole vacuum humor bit to be a little gross, except I know Grandma would have thought it was pretty darn funny," Mary Jane interjected. "You kids help Grandpa finish unpacking. I've got to finish making dinner. It'll be ready about six o'clock."

7

Jim Viejo

PRESENT TIMES

VIEJO STABBED A THICK SLICE OF PORK ROAST WITH HIS fork and sliced off a bite-size piece with his steak knife. The meat was tender and juicy. The home-made gravy imparted a smoky flavor to the meat and mashed potatoes. Mary Jane was a wonderful chef, and he was looking forward to some excellent home-cooked meals after subsisting primarily on a diet of Marine menu and fast-food takeout since Betti's passing. The warm comfort of being with his family seated around the table was beginning to make him feel connected to life again, giving hope that the emotional turmoil inside him would eventually work its way out. Time, he guessed, was the answer, but he also understood that healing was going to require a continuous conscious effort on his part. He had always stood up to any enemy. This enemy was inside him . . . could he stand up to himself?

"Hey, Grandpa," Meghan said between mouthfuls. "I got a surprise for you."

"Oh, and what, pray tell, is that?"

"There's someone I want you to meet. She's single, smart, and gorgeous. Her name is Renee Romero, and she's one of my law professors at the university."

Momentary dread gripped Viejo. He wasn't ready to meet someone new. Not yet anyway.

"Before you freak out, Grandpa, it's not like I'm setting you up for a date," Meghan said.

"Sure sounds like it," Peyton said, laughing nervously and glancing over at his wife with a smile.

"No, it's nothing like that," Meghan said. "She just wants to meet you. I told her you were retiring from the Marines, and that you're moving here to be close to family. I figured what with your being new in town, it would be nice to start out knowing someone right away. Probably doesn't hurt that she's kinda hot."

Viejo thought about that for a long moment, struggling to decide how to respond to his granddaughter's thoughtful gesture. "Hot? I've been out of the game so long, maybe I should start with someone who's lukewarm."

The family burst out laughing at Viejo's response. "Looks like you brought some of that famous corny old 'Grandpa Jim humor' along with you, Dad. Glad to see it. I've really missed it."

"I've arranged for you to sit in on a special lecture about the reliability of witness testimony. Should be pretty cool," Meghan said. "Lecture's tomorrow at eleven."

Viejo sighed, stabbed another piece of pork, and slowly chewed it. When he finished swallowing, he patted his lips with his napkin and said, "Well, as long as you're not trying to play Cupid with me, I suppose it could be interesting to sit in on the lecture. And to meet Renee Romero."

"Fantastic!" Meghan said enthusiastically. "It's settled then."

After dinner, Viejo excused himself, pleading the need to recover from the long day of driving. He changed into his pajamas, got into bed, and, as usual, thoughts of Betti came. He recalled their last conversation in her hospital room the night before she passed.

Betti had managed a weak smile. "Not much time left, Jim. Don't feel sorry for me. I couldn't imagine a better life or a better husband. I would choose you again every time. My greatest fear is that you will roll up in a ball and be lonely the rest of your life. Not to be morbid, but I have been thinking that instead of an urn, I want you to keep my ashes in that music box you bought me for our tenth anniversary . . . you know, the one which plays our special song, 'Somewhere Over the Rainbow.' Whenever you need to, play the music, and know that I am somewhere over the rainbow, sending down my love. Carry my ashes as long as you want but set me free when you know it's time."

"That time won't EVER come, Betti! I've never so much as had a thought about any other woman since the day we met. I can't bear the thought of losing you. No one will ever take your place in my heart."

"Nor your place in mine. I'm not asking you to give my place in your heart to anyone. I want you to allow some very special person to find their own place in your heart. When this happens, you'll know it's time to set me free, and please, please believe with all your heart that wherever I am, I'll be happy for you and grateful for the happiness she brings you."

Betti drifted into unconscientiousness. Those were the last words she ever spoke.

Viejo leaned across to the nightstand, wound the key to Betti's music box, and drifted off to sleep to the sound of their song.

8

Jim Viejo & Renee Romero
PRESENT DAY

THE CAMPUS CAFÉ BUSTLED WITH ACTIVITY IN THE mid-morning rush. The sound of multiple conversations and the clink of silverware on plates filled the dining area as servers rushed from table to table, taking orders and bringing out plates of food from the kitchen. Viejo gazed around him at the young students. The energy radiating in the room was invigorating. He smiled at Meghan, who sat across the table from him. Two of her close friends and fellow law school classmates, Maureen Berruti and Barb Henthorn, joined them at the table. Viejo thought he might feel awkward hanging with three beautiful coeds, but he didn't. He enjoyed playing the role of a mellow old grandfather.

The girls and he exchanged typical small talk over mugs of steaming coffee accompanied by doughnuts and frosted Danish.

"What was it like being in the Marines for so many years?" Barb asked.

"Months of boredom, punctuated by moments of terror," Viejo replied while pushing brief flashbacks of combat out of his head. "We're designed for combat, you know. We are expected to put our lives on the line and always have each other's backs."

"It must've been terrible during the first Gulf War," Maureen inserted. "I assume you were there?"

"Yeah, he was there," Meghan said. "My grandpa was in almost every armed conflict the United States has been involved with since he served in Vietnam."

"Oh, wow!" Barb exclaimed. "You're a regular old war hero!"

"Far from it," Viejo said, feeling uncomfortable and wanting to change the subject. "I just did my duty like everyone else. But you got the old part right."

Meghan glanced at her watch. "Oh, shoot! Look at the time! We gotta get to class. Don't want to be late."

The girls gathered their class materials as they stood up. Viejo laid money on the table to pay the bill, along with a generous tip.

"I got to hit the head," he said.

"Head?" Maureen asked, puzzled.

"That's Marine for bathroom."

Meghan said, laughing, "Always thought that was a weird word for bathroom. You would think they would use another body part to describe it."

"Maybe you can suggest another term," Viejo said, joining in the laughter. "Would be hard to do it and keep a PG rating, though. I'll give it some thought. The Marines I've known haven't been particularly sensitive, so I won't waste time trying for a PG rating."

Meghan giggled. "Okay, we'll see you in there! I'll save a seat for you."

"See you there," Viejo replied as he rose from his seat.

* * *

Renee Romero sat behind the desk in her office, eyeing the two large young men sitting in front of her. They sat nervously, fidgeting with the black ski masks in their laps, obviously excited about their role this morning.

"Looks to me like the drama department did a great job of typecasting with you guys. No offense, but you do look like a couple of tough goons. Now, you know how this has to work, right? You have to be as loud, frightening, and believable as possible. I want this to be a very memorable experience."

"Don't worry Professor Romero. Zack and I rehearsed this until past midnight. We will stay out of sight and burst in at exactly 10:17."

Satisfied with the response, Romero held up her wristwatch and had them synchronize with her watch. "Be scary!"

"Don't worry, Ma'am. We'll be scarier than a blind date with a math major!"

* * *

Romero entered the lecture hall, pleased to see that she had nearly full attendance. The students had all been prepped for what was about to happen. She'd warned them that fake robbers were going to burst into the classroom to stage a mock holdup. The students were supposed to record their observations of the experience. A banker friend of hers was kind enough to provide the standard form that bank managers hand out to employees after a robbery. The form featured a blank figure of a person and spaces to fill in, describing each feature of the person. They were instructed to fill out the form later and, most importantly, not to confer with one another about what they had seen.

Romero walked to the podium and turned the mic on. She opened her briefcase and removed several files. Opening one, she studied her lecture notes for a few moments while the class settled down.

Clearing her throat, she said, "Good morning, future champions of truth and justice!"

Groans and slight laughter from the class.

"This morning, we are going to talk about witnesses. As we all know, testimony from witnesses is the single most determining factor influencing the jury's verdict. It follows that the handling of witnesses is undoubtedly the most challenging trial component for a trial lawyer.

Friday's lecture will cover techniques for dealing with hostile witnesses and other witnesses testifying for the opposing side. Today, I am going to focus on dealing with your own witnesses.

"Let's start with the most important rule. After you have reviewed depositions and considered your trial strategy, you must carefully coach your witness on what to say, as well as on what not to say. Never, ever ask your witness a question unless you know the answer in advance. The last thing you want is a big surprise from your own witness!"

Suddenly, the two actors, wearing masks and holding prop pistols from the drama department, threw open the lecture hall doors and ran toward the front of the class, waving the pistols wildly, looking for all the world like drug-crazed robbers. The larger of the two held a canvas grocery bag in his non-pistol hand.

"This is a robbery! Everyone put your wallets and cellphones in this bag!" the bag holder shouted, holding up the bag. "Do it quickly, and nobody gets hurt!"

His cohort began walking along the front row as students complied, putting their wallets and cellphones in the canvas bag.

Romero grinned, noting the startled looks from the students, even though they knew the robbery was just an exercise. She heard the lecture hall doors fly open off to her right, and glancing over, she saw a man with grayish-black hair bolt through the door and run at the lead robber, grabbing him by the neck in a choke hold and twisting his wrist until he dropped the weapon. He wheeled around and delivered a karate kick to the midsection of the other fake robber, who went down like a sack of potatoes.

"Stop! Stop!" Romero screamed, running out from behind the podium and getting between the man and the two actors.

The guy looked at her with a confused look on his face.

"This is just a class demonstration!" Romero blurted, waving her hands in a protective gesture. "It wasn't real. I hope these two aren't seriously injured!"

"Oh, my god!" the man replied, his face turning red. "It looked pretty real to me. I thought everyone was in danger. It looked like these two crazies were about to start shooting."

Romero, regaining her composure as her adrenaline rush began to diminish, asked the actors if they needed medical attention. They both declined. The larger one said his wrist was a little sore, and the other apparently only had the wind knocked out of him and said he was fully recovered. Oddly enough, they both said they took to experience as being highly complementary of their acting skills. The man apologized profusely. They shook his hand, said there were no hard feelings, and left, no doubt in a hurry to share their tale with the entire drama department.

"I'm so, so sorry for messing up your lecture. I'm Jim Viejo, by the way. Meghan's grandpa."

"I thought so," she said, offering her hand. "Renee Romero."

"Nice to meet you. If you will take that empty seat next to Meghan, I'll try to get things back under control."

Romero returned to the podium. "Everyone, take your seats."

"Okay, now that all the excitement is over," Romero said as the class settled down, "we can get on with the lecture."

She couldn't help but glance over at Meghan and her grandpa. He was as strikingly handsome as Meghan had said he was, and he was obviously heroic. Not knowing what was happening, he'd thrown himself into harm's way, risking his life for the safety of other people.

"I apologize for any trauma some of you may have just experienced. What you have seen is an exercise gone horribly wrong. It was supposed to give you a very memorable experience of being a witness yourself. This time, it was considerably more memorable than I had intended. Nevertheless, we are going to follow through with the assignment. I want each of you, without discussing what happened with any of your classmates, to fill out the witness forms I handed out during the last lecture. I assume you studied them and knew what features to look for regarding robbers."

She paused, scanning the room. Everyone was focused on her.

"At our next class, we will go over the forms. I believe you will be surprised at how different the individual accounts will be, all from people who saw essentially the same thing at the same time. I believe you will gain a better perspective about how unreliable witnesses can be. This is an important point to consider when evaluating testimony from witnesses. The fact of the matter is that witness testimony is seldom completely accurate. There are generally cracks in their testimony which you can use to your advantage, or if need be, cover over so they can't be used to your disadvantage. Okay, class dismissed. Meghan, I would like to meet with you and your guest in my office."

* * *

Romero leaned back in her chair and gazed intently at Meghan and Viejo, sitting across from the desk in her office. She folded both hands in front of her and tried to summon a stern look but was failing miserably. She began to giggle, noting the relieved expressions on the two faces in front of her.

"Oh, my god!" she squealed. "That was the funniest thing ever to happen in law class!"

"Again, I'm so sorry," Viejo said. "I honestly thought the robbery was real."

"You were supposed to," Meghan said. "Then you went all Rambo on those poor drama students. Must've scared the crap out of 'em."

Meghan started laughing, and Viejo joined in.

"Really, in all seriousness," Romero said, "it's a good thing you didn't hurt those kids. But be that as it may, if a lawsuit for damages were to come out of this, I would have to testify that I personally instructed those two young men to make their attack look as real and scary as possible. It's not your fault that you bought their performance. They were paid to make everyone buy it. I'll offer to triple their fees. I suspect that will be the end of it, although this will probably make them legends in the drama department."

"I hope so," Viejo said. "I don't want to cause you any trouble."

"Don't worry, I cause enough all by myself."

As she sat across from Viejo, it occurred to Renee that she found him attractive. When Meghan told her about her grandpa, she'd known that her student was playing matchmaker, and she didn't mind. It was becoming more and more obvious that her relationship with Howard had never been more than just a matter of convenience and wasn't destined to be permanent. The timing seemed right to move on, and here was this obviously very interesting alternative right in front of her.

She thought back to what Father Herb mentioned to her the other day when she told him she wanted to increase her volunteer time at the clinic. He'd said that help was on the way, help with the clinic and the gangs. Could this man be the help he said was coming? She wasn't sure, but she figured it would be good to find out.

Romero shot Meghan a conspiratorial smile and turned to Viejo.

"I know we just met, but I have an idea I would like to share with you. It might be something you would be interested in pursuing. Can I buy you a drink later while we talk?"

"I'm sure I can work you into my extremely busy non-schedule. I had planned to do some apartment hunting, but there's no real rush on that." He didn't hesitate to say, "I'd be happy to have a drink with you, and I promise not to beat up the bartender."

The women laughed at his response. Meghan wore a smug grin, her mission accomplished.

"Great! Meet you around six o'clock at Two Fools Tavern on Central."

"Two Fools? Anything significant about that?" Viejo asked.

"We'll just have to see, won't we?"

Meghan stood up from her chair.

"Come on, Grandpa. Let's get out of Professor Romero's hair."

Viejo stood up, as did Romero.

"Looking forward to tonight," he said, turning to leave with Meghan.

Gazing out the window, Renee couldn't believe she had been so spontaneous. Had she really asked Jim Viejo what could be construed as a "date" after just meeting him, literally just minutes ago? Was she that desperate?

9

Betti

FOR THE FIRST TIME SINCE MY DEATH, I FINALLY HAVE a tiny spark of hope for my troubled husband. His long overdue decision to retire from the Corps indicates that he knows he has to deal with his problems and get on with his life. Jim was always one to take responsibility. Illogical as it seems, his natural reaction to losing Michael and me was to assume that he was responsible. That his actions led to being punished by God. Five years of wallowing in this absurd, misguided notion have taken its toll. I am hoping he will find someone to lead him out of his self-imposed misery. Finding love again is a much-preferred remedy to his condition than drugs or alcohol will ever provide. They only offer a brief respite, not a cure.

I'm watching him get ready for the first encounter resembling a date he's had since I died. I'm thrilled for him and hopeful this law professor our granddaughter has set him up with won't break his fragile heart. Meghan is a good judge of character. I have faith in her. She wouldn't set Jim up with a toxic person.

I hear him talking to me. My music box sits on top of the nightstand adjacent to his bed, and he's paused in front of it in nothing but his boxer shorts. He winds up the music box and plays "Somewhere Over the Rainbow," likely in an effort to soften the guilt he is feeling from opening the door for another woman to enter his life.

"I don't know if I'm ready for this," he says, gently stroking the side of the music box. "I know Meghan means well, but this could be a disaster waiting to happen."

I want to tell him not to worry, but sadly, I can't from my self-requested state of limbo. I can make him feel me, though, and that alone might give him the ability to go out and have a good time for once.

"Meghan and Mary Jane are definitely playing matchmaker," Viejo says, moving across the room to put on a button-down short-sleeve plaid shirt. "I guess that's okay; I know they're just trying to help. Meghan says this isn't a date, but it sure feels like it."

I watch as Viejo opens the middle dresser drawer and pulls out a pair of blue jeans. He puts them on and then dons a pair of casual shoes. I'm pleased to see he's taking the time to look nice. Nothing fancy. Viejo never was one to put on airs. He simply is who he is. Take it or leave it. Another one of his challenging but lovable components is his rugged individualism, his lack of the need to impress others. He always was his own man.

As I continue to watch, Jim combs his hair, slaps on a few drops of aftershave, and shrugs on a light windbreaker, apparently to guard against the nighttime spring chill.

He's about to leave the bedroom when he stops dead in his tracks, turns and goes into the bathroom, stopping in front of the medicine cabinet. After staring at himself in the mirror, he opens the cabinet door and removes an almost full bottle of valium. My heart sinks.

"No, no, no!" I want to scream. I don't. He can't hear me.

He taps two pills into his left palm and stares at them for a long moment.

"Don't you dare!"

"I know you're disappointed in me, Betti," he says, eyeing the pills. He pushes them around in his palm with his right index finger. He picks one up and is about to swallow it, but then he stops. "And I don't want you to be."

I want to do a dance of joy when I see him drop the two pills back into the bottle, seal the bottle, and put it back in the medicine cabinet. I can tell he's already gaining inner strength as a result of the move, and I'm overjoyed about it. I want only for him to find happiness in life again, and I'm hopeful he might have a shot at it with this law professor.

"You know," he says, looking around, "it's almost like you're standing right next to me, Betti. I can almost feel you, almost smell your favorite perfume. I love you dearly. I always, always will."

Am I really getting through that strongly? I wonder.

He looks at his watch and hurries out of the bathroom. I smile as I watch him leave.

10

Jim Viejo
PRESENT TIMES

VIEJO SLOWLY SIPPED A GUINNESS STOUT FROM A pint glass in the dimly lit Two Fools Tavern. He'd chosen a booth at the far end of the room, hoping for some privacy. He'd arrived a little early so he wouldn't be late for what surely did feel like a date, even though Meghan had assured him it wasn't. Not wanting to disappoint his granddaughter, he played along with her plan, but wasn't really certain he wanted to be there, sailing into unfamiliar waters, wary as to where this might lead. By all appearances, Renee Romero was a smart, successful, and attractive woman. Given his issues, he wasn't confident that he was ready to be in a relationship, and he certainly didn't want to go through the pain associated with a messy breakup. Did he need to do more personal work on himself before he could venture into a relationship? At worst, the evening could serve as a test to determine if he was capable of something as simple as holding up his end in an engaging conversation with another woman.

He glanced at his watch and saw it was six o'clock. He looked toward the door and smiled as he watched Romero saunter in. She wore a tight-fitting, low-cut blouse and black leather boots that came up her calves, accentuating the tight fit of her jeans. She had a light jacket slung over her shoulder. Spotting him, she came over, smiling broadly as he stood up to greet her.

"You certainly are punctual," Viejo said, offering her his hand. "I like that. Marines are always on time."

"I bet they are."

Romero laughed, shook his hand, unslung the purse from her shoulder, and sat down across the table from him.

"Any more heroics since this morning?" she asked.

"I was tempted to leap a tall building with a single bound on the way over here, but I thought I might sprain an ankle if I landed on a loose piece of kryptonite."

"You're pretty glib for a Marine."

"Yeah, it's probably why I never made general. Glib doesn't go over too well in the Corps."

"It doesn't go over well in court either."

A server arrived at the table to take their drink order.

"It would be borderline criminal to order anything but a Guinness in an Irish bar, wouldn't it?" she asked playfully.

"No, not a crime," said the server. "But Guinness on draft is our specialty." The server turned to Viejo. "And for you, sir?"

"Lady's both a judge and a law professor . . . gotta be an expert on criminal activity. I guess if it's criminal not to order Guinness, I'll have another as well."

"Smart choice," the server said and hurried off to get their drinks.

They exchanged small talk as they studied the menu. The waiter returned with their beers, and they ordered dinner—a shepherd's pie for Viejo and salmon on steamed rice for Romero.

"I'm glad you could join me tonight," Romero said. "Meghan has told me so much about you. I feel like I already know you."

"That gives you an unfair advantage."

"That it does!" Romero smiled.

Viejo realized he was feeling unexpectedly comfortable in her presence. Surprising, as he hadn't had anything remotely resembling a social outing since Betti died.

"So, tell me a little about yourself," Viejo said. "Seems only fair to level the playing field a little."

Romero leaned back in her chair, lifted the tall glass of Guinness, and took a long pull.

"Ah, hits the spot," she said.

They remained silent for a long moment, Romero obviously trying to decide where to start. She took another pull on the beer and began. "My story isn't nearly as exciting as yours. No traveling the world. No medals for bravery. Born and raised here in Albuquerque. My parents were both schoolteachers. Dad is a full-blooded Hispanic. Mom, as Irish as they come. Both are Catholic to the bone. Mostly for financial purposes, I decided to go to college at UNM to cut expenses. Majored in sociology and was going to be a do-gooder-saver-of-the-world, but I found out after graduation that none of the local employers were interested in hiring somebody to save the world. Thus, the default choice was to go to law school with all the other young graduates who weren't clever enough to major in something you could actually leverage into a job."

He nodded at her, encouraging her to continue.

"The city's legal department hired me right out of law school. There wasn't much money. But lots of trial experience. A few years later, I used my trial experience to land a job as a litigator with one of the local law firms. About ten years ago, my uncle, who was a district judge, had some health issues and needed to retire before his term expired. He used some connections to get me appointed to fill out his term. When the term expired, I ran for election and have managed to get myself reelected every time since then. Voters don't pay much attention to judge elections. You're pretty much a shoo-in for reelection if you don't commit an axe murder or get drunk and run over a busload of kids."

"You didn't mention your personal life."

"Cause there hasn't been much to shout about, and what there has been is mostly painful. I thought I had found my prince charming in one of the partners at the law firm. We were married for over twenty years. He never wanted kids, so as we grew older, we never developed that family glue to hold us together. It's a classic case of drifting apart, combined with an extremely attractive, gold-digging legal assistant he hired and then ran off with two years ago. In reflection, I don't think he ever was fully committed to me. He was probably cheating behind my back all along. If he had managed to stay with me 'til death do us part,' the jerk probably would have brought a date to my funeral. Even though I realize I'm much better off without him, it still hurts pretty bad. Oh well, as it says in the Bible, 'This, too, shall pass.'"

"Yeah, but what they don't tell you is that sometimes it passes like a ten-pound kidney stone! My wife died five years ago, and I still miss her every day."

Romero, raising her glass, said, "Here's to smaller kidney stones!"

"Amen to that."

"As you might surmise from the Bible reference, I've always been a fairly spiritual person," Romero said. "I don't go to church every Sunday, but I believe in God, a higher power we have to accept on faith."

"I think I'm on God's shit list," Viejo said, immediately regretting his candor.

He saw the surprise register on Romero's face.

"Why is that?"

"Don't want to talk about it."

"Fair enough," she said, letting it go.

He liked the fact that she didn't push him.

The server arrived with their food. After he left and they began eating, Viejo asked, "So you became a lawyer by default? What did you really want to do?"

"I thought about a career as a therapist when I was an undergraduate. I had the strange idea that I could be a positive influence in the world. Make a difference, you know?"

"I understand. But life threw a monkey wrench into your plans?"

"As I said, my sociology degree didn't open any doors. My parents were great, but we didn't have much money, so I had to work my way through school and take out student loans as well. Money became a key motivator. The legal profession offered the best alternative to climb out of my financial hole. I rationalized with myself that I could make good money and still pursue my do-gooder instincts as a lawyer. Now, all these years later, I'm not so sure. The system has become so polluted. It has devolved into a system designed primarily to generate money for insurance companies and lawyers. The occasional justice rendered is just an unanticipated by-product. I thought getting the bad guys off the streets would make a positive difference, but, in the end, the damned court system is set up like a revolving door. Bad guys get arrested, charged, and released. It's very frustrating. The only bright spot for me is my teaching gig at UNM. Academia is so much more idyllic and enjoyable than the real world. The bright young minds recharge my battery. My admittedly Pollyanna hope is that I can be a positive influence on the new generations of lawyers, inspiring them to make changes in the system. Make it more like our founding fathers intended."

"Sounds like you'd like to spend more time teaching and less time on the bench," Viejo responded.

"That's why I am resigning from my judgeship. I'm tired of riding this merry-go-round."

"What are you going to do now? Take on more classes at the university?"

"I want to teach more, but not full time," Romero replied. "I'm also going to increase my volunteer hours at Holy Mother's Clinic."

"Holy Mother?"

Romero told him all about the clinic, Father Herb, and the severe problems associated with teenage pregnancy, particularly in gang-infested neighborhoods. She mentioned the increasing gang activity near the clinic and the threat the gangs posed to the clinic.

"Can't the cops crack down on the bad actors?" Viejo asked.

"They try. But they can't be everywhere at once. The bangers know that, so the problems just keep coming. Assaults, rapes, robberies, prostitution, and, of course, drugs, drugs, drugs, drugs! I hate drugs! They destroy countless lives. Turn addicts into criminals. They're the root of the other crimes."

Viejo suddenly felt uncomfortable. Thinking about his probable addiction to valium, he said nothing, feeling hypocritical as he nodded in agreement.

"Anyway," Romero said, "I asked you here for a reason."

Viejo raised an eyebrow. "Really? I thought we were just getting to know each other."

"We are, but I have an ulterior motive for luring you here tonight. You see, I thought being new in town you might want something positive to do with your time. We need more of a male influence at the clinic. All the paid staff and volunteers are female. The only man in the entire operation is Father Herb, who, as a priest, doesn't fit the traditional male role model. The kids, especially the boys, need a positive male role model to emulate. I was wondering if that kind of thing might interest a big, tough old Marine like you."

"You got the old part right. I just turned fifty-eight last month."

Romero laughed. "Fifty-eight isn't old. Besides, I'm fifty-five, so you're callin' me old! Not nice, Jim. Not nice at all."

"What would I be doing there?"

"You good at math?"

"I graduated from NMSU with a degree in mechanical engineering. So, yeah, I'm good at math."

"Math is a major area of weakness for many of the kids. They don't have educated parents to help or motivate them. Hell, most only have mothers, and many of those mothers are not much more than kids themselves. The problem is made even worse when teenage boys take pride in getting their girlfriends pregnant. They see impregnating a girl as a rite of passage, a symbol of their virility. They call their victims, and that's what they are, 'baby mamas.' Can you believe that?"

"Baby mamas, eh?" he asked, finishing the last of his pie. "That's pretty pathetic."

"Yeah, it is. We need you. The clinic can save these kids. Promise me you'll think about it?"

Viejo turned the idea of volunteering at a youth clinic over in his mind. Doing volunteer work had never occurred to him. He thought it might be good for him to get his mind off his own troubles in favor of helping others overcome theirs.

"I'll give the idea some thought," Viejo answered, nodding his head. "Might be good for me for many reasons."

"Giving back is always better than taking," Romero said. "Would you like to see the place? Meet Father Herb? I think once you've seen the clinic for yourself, you'll understand how vital it is for the neighborhood and what a critical difference you could make."

"Can't hurt to go take a look," Viejo said. "Not like I'd have to juggle my schedule to accommodate this little excursion. Matter of fact, by no coincidence at all, I just happen to be free tomorrow. The only thing on my plate for the next few days is trying to find a place to live. As much as I love May Jane and her family, I've got to have my own space."

"Excellent," Romero said. "I'll pick you up at ten, and afterward, I'll buy lunch at Henry Apodaca's World-Famous Taco Cafe."

"You had me at 'buy!'" Viejo said, laughing. "Serving as a district judge, teaching at law school, volunteering at the clinic. Doesn't seem like you have much time for yourself. How do you decompress? Surely, you allow a little time for yourself."

"As a matter of fact, I do have a hobby of sorts. I'm a hot-air balloon pilot. An old friend and I bought a used balloon a few years ago. It's exhilarating to take it up. We try to take it for a flight at least once a month. It's in the shop right now, having new burners installed. It should be ready next week. Would you like to fly with me sometime?"

"Can't honestly say that a hot-air balloon ride is on my bucket list, but what the hell, I'm all about new experiences."

They spent the rest of the evening in pleasant conversation, sharing mostly humorous stories from past adventures and misadventures. Glancing at her watch, Romero was surprised to see it was almost eleven o'clock.

"Oh, my gosh! I can't believe it's this late. I have to get home and review my notes for an early morning class."

"Let me pay the bill, and I'll walk you to your car. It's getting pretty late for this old Marine as well."

As they walked to her car, Viejo experienced a sense of unease, typical for a guy contemplating the proper way to end a first date. His problem was compounded by the length of time it had been since he had done anything like this, as well as not knowing if this really *was* a date. *A hug? A light peck on the cheek?* He decided to play it safe and offer a handshake. Romero seemed to feel the awkwardness as well, but she shook his hand, holding on a little longer than he expected.

Driving home, he thought about how comfortable the evening had been. It surprised him. He'd just met the woman. Could this be leading somewhere he wasn't prepared to go? Or to something he desperately needed? Mary Jane had never mentioned a curfew. He hoped he wasn't going to cause a problem with his late return. After arriving, he went to unlock the front door, fumbling with the keys. He tried to enter without disturbing anybody, but as he crossed the threshold, his daughter's dachshund started barking.

"Might have known there would be a sentry. At ease, Tootie. Friend, not foe, friend, not foe."

He patted the dog on the head and went upstairs to get ready for bed. He got into his pajamas and headed for the bathroom to brush his teeth. Looking in the mirror, he realized he had a goofy grin on his face, one he hadn't seen in quite some time.

11

Jim Viejo
PRESENT TIMES

V IEJO SAT ON MARY JANE'S FRONT PORCH, ENJOYING the cool, sunny Albuquerque morning. He thought he could easily adapt to the famous Albuquerque climate, featuring an average of 310 sunny days per year.

He glanced at his watch. Five minutes to ten. Romero pulled up in front of the house at exactly ten o'clock. Her green Lexus was impressive. He had barely noticed it when he walked her out in the dark last night. The driver's side window went down as he approached the car.

"Hey, big guy!" Romero said, beaming at him. "You ready to rumble?"

Viejo grinned as he opened the front passenger side door, got in, and buckled up.

"I certainly am! I'm looking forward to touring the clinic almost as much as the free lunch you offered."

"And so you shall. Touring and tacos should be one helluva a day," Romero grinned, pulling away from the curb.

"Nice car," Viejo said casually. "Must've cost you a fortune."

Romero glanced over at him and smiled. "It did. I think I mentioned that I left the prosecutor's office to go into corporate law before I became a judge?"

"Why yes, I recall you did."

"Yeah, I went over to the dark side to make a boatload of money. I invested my earnings wisely. The dot-com bubble got me real good, but my portfolio is recovering."

"I don't own stocks."

"Less than half of Americans do," Romero said. "Anyway, to continue, the cheating ex-husband I told you about was forced into a very substantial divorce settlement."

"Hell hath no fury . . ." Viejo said.

"I'm currently dating an accountant. A guy by the name of Howard. He's helped me with my financial strategy."

Oddly, Viejo felt a pang of jealousy, which he knew was absurd. He'd only just met Romero.

"You guys serious?" he asked.

"Howard thinks we are. I'm not really sure whether the relationship will last. Truth be told, he's more of a comfortable convenience than anything else."

"Whoa! Harsh! You'd tell that to a veritable stranger? Which is what I am."

"Somehow, I feel like I know you. Like I said, I feel like I can trust you. Isn't that weird? We only just met."

"Thanks for the kind words. But you may not feel that way once you get to know me better."

"Guess I'll just have to take my chances."

They left the Northeast Heights and headed toward the west side of the city. As they neared the Five Points area, Viejo noted how the surroundings declined from pleasant suburban to barrio urban decay in short order. It always struck him how neighborhoods only a few blocks away from each other could be so totally different. One a decent place to live, the other a living hell full of gun violence, poverty, and despair.

"Boy, what a difference a few blocks can make," Viejo said. "I feel like I should be wearing my sidearm."

"Isn't it sad?" Romero said.

She pointed at a park they were passing. It was obviously a hangout for hookers, addicts, and drug dealers.

"This is part of what I wanted you to see," Romero continued. "When I was a little girl, my grandparents owned a little house near here. I spent a lot of time with them, playing in the park, walking to the ice cream parlor, and all that kinda stuff. It was a nice older part of town. Mom-and-pop businesses flourished. People weren't afraid to walk the streets. In fact, we used to have picnics in that park. Now look at it. It's going to get nothing but worse if we can't run the gangs out of here."

"I'm afraid the gangs are probably here to stay, Renee."

"You might be right, but we have to try to make things better for whomever we can."

Viejo laughed a belly laugh.

"What's so funny?"

"Whomever? Boy, I haven't heard that word used in casual conversation . . . well, maybe never!"

Romero laughed along with Viejo.

"I told you. Both my parents were schoolteachers. They made sure we spoke proper English, along with Spanish, in our home. They were sticklers, kind of like grammar Nazis. Okay, we're here."

Romero parked near the front door of the clinic, next to a big, shiny white Harley. The motorcycle looked vaguely familiar to Viejo. They got out of the car and headed toward the entrance of the clinic. Romero spotted a group of gangbangers approaching.

"This can't be good," Romero muttered. "These guys are bad news, Jim. Especially that big guy, the one with all the tats. Name's Roque Sanchez. He's one of the gang leaders around here."

Viejo looked from Romero to Roque.

"Back yet again, Judge?" Roque asked, standing a little too close to her. "I told you bad things happen to good people around here. Why don't you go back to where you belong?"

Viejo didn't like the guy's tone of voice, nor that he was standing too close to Romero, obviously in an effort to intimidate her. The young thug towered over her.

Romero appeared undaunted. "Like I've told you before, you really don't want to mess with me if you know what's good for you. Now, why don't you step back and let us pass?"

"Do as the lady says," Viejo snarled, stepping closer to Roque.

"And who the hell do you think you are?" Roque asked, his voice menacing.

"An ex-Marine who's gonna kick your ass if you don't back off right now."

Viejo saw the anger flash across the banger's face, noting the evil behind his dead eyes. Another man might have been scared, but not Viejo. Roque clenched his fists. Not used to being challenged. Summoning some extra bravado, he turned to his compadres.

"You get this guy? Thinks he can kick my ass!"

The group all laughed. One of them said, "Yeah, like that's gonna happen. Yeah, you and what army?"

Viejo got in Roque's face and growled, "Don't need an army, just one tough old Marine. Mess with me and you'll leave here in an ambulance!"

Roque backed off, swaggering away. Saving face, he shouted back, "You're one lucky geezer, man! Good for you, I ain't got time to fool with you today. Maybe next time!"

Once inside, Romero turned to Viejo and thanked him for interceding.

"You see how much we need you around here?" she said, her voice low and full of emotion. "I know I should feel sorry for them, but I really hate those scumbags. They want to drag everyone down to their miserable level."

"Too bad their parents weren't into birth control," Viejo responded as they approached the front desk.

"Jim, this is Jessie," Romero said, nodding toward Jessie, who was seated at her usual spot behind the front desk. "Jessie, this is Jim. He's thinking about volunteering here."

Jessie shook Viejo's hand and welcomed him to the clinic.

"I haven't committed yet," he said with a laugh. "I'm in the thinking stage. Just getting the lay of the land is all. You get harassed when you come here?" he asked.

Jessie sighed. "Yeah, almost every day. The gangs don't like us. They want things to stay the way they are."

"Well, they've got another think coming," Romero said. "Come on, Jim. I'll introduce you to Father Herb."

Viejo accompanied her down a narrow hall with classrooms on either side. Most of the rooms were full of teenage boys and girls, primarily girls, who were studying under the guidance of teachers while other students studied on their own.

Romero stopped at the open door of Father Herb's office and knocked on the jamb. Turning away from his computer screen, Father Herb spun around in his swivel chair, a big grin on his face. Viejo was stunned. It was the guy on the motorcycle—the crazy dude from the Winnebago encounter.

"Well, look what the cat dragged in!" Grinning widely, Father Herb stood up, came around his desk, and offered Viejo his hand. "Nice to meet you again, Colonel Viejo."

"You guys know each other?" Romero asked, incredulous.

Momentarily speechless, Viejo shook Father Herb's hand. He swallowed hard and said, "You're the guy I met on I-40 the day before yesterday. The guy on the motorcycle who helped the old couple in the Winnebago with the flat tire."

"One and the same," Father Herb said, patting Viejo on the back. "Thanks for taking the time to come along with Renee this morning."

Something about Father Herb was strangely soothing. He exuded serenity. His eyes revealed a kindness, representing the antithesis of what he'd seen in the eyes of the gangbangers in front of the clinic. Viejo and Romero sat down in the two chairs in front of Herb's desk. Judging from the office, it appeared the clinic's budget did not allow much for creature comforts. A wooden crucifix hanging on the wall behind Father Herb was the only decoration. Other than their chairs, what appeared to be a military surplus desk, gray metal filing cabinets, a coat rack, and a single bookshelf holding a few books on it were the only furnishings.

"I can't believe you've met before!" Romero said. "What an amazing coincidence! Father Herb, I've asked Jim to come here to see what we're doing to improve the quality of life in the neighborhood, especially for the unwed teen moms."

"Jesus! This is all just too much of a coincidence," Viejo said, obviously unnerved at the unexpected encounter with the priest.

"One of my best friends. Jesus." Father Herb smiled, not sounding as if he were joking. "I hope to introduce you to Him. Not in heaven. But while you're here on earth."

"Jim says he might want to volunteer here," Romero said. "You see, he's just retired from the Marines and—."

"He's moved back here to be with his family," Father Herb said, finishing her sentence. "Yes, I'm well aware."

Viejo was starting to wonder if he had stumbled into another dimension. This all was too surreal. His thoughts were interrupted by a tap on the door. Viejo looked over his shoulder and saw a boy, about age twelve but big for his years, standing at the threshold. From his demeanor and speech, he was obviously mentally challenged.

"Do, da yous want somethin' to drink?" the boy asked.

"No, thanks, Billy. We're about to take this gentleman on the nickel tour of the place. Maybe we'll want something later," Father Herb said, his voice reflecting obvious affection for the youngster.

Billy left, smiling broadly as he backed out of the office.

"That's Jessie's kid," Father Herb said. "The young lady at the front desk."

"Yeah, Jim met her when we came in," Romero said. "Uh, Roque and his crew were at it again. They're intimidating everyone who comes in here. It's just got to stop, Father Herb. This is intolerable. It's just going to escalate if we don't do something!"

The look on Father Herb's face evidenced that the priest was struggling to hold back an unpriestly response.

Viejo pitched in. "Yeah, the guy was getting up into Renee's face. She wasn't going to back down. But I was about to open up a fair-sized can of whip-ass, excuse the language."

"Jim rattled his cage pretty hard. Roque's like most bullies. He took off after Jim stood up to him."

"I'm going to contact Detective Fermin Padilla. The Albuquerque Police Department PD has got to start giving us better protection," Father Herb said. "We've got to put a stop to this."

"Could stir up trouble, you know," Viejo said. "If the cops make life hard for the gangs, they'll turn around and make life hard for you. I'm not saying you shouldn't do anything to stop them, but just be aware there would likely be repercussions."

"Point well taken," Romero said. "Plus, they know that the cops can't be here all the time, or even most of the time. We're always going to be vulnerable."

Father Herb nodded. "I'm calling Fermin anyway. Maybe he will have some ideas."

Father Herb stood up from his desk. "Let's get going. Renee and I will give you the nickel tour. In gratitude for your helping Renee today, I'll waive the nickel fee."

"Fee waiver and free lunch. This is turning into quite a day!" Viejo grinned.

They showed Viejo around, all the while filling him in on what they did for the youth they served. Everything from basic tutoring to prepping for the GED test, to learning home and life skills, and mastering basic computer skills. They stopped in a classroom empty except for a guitar teacher and her two students.

"Hi, Maria," Father Herb said, entering the classroom with Viejo and Romero. "How's the lesson going today?"

Maria smiled. "With such excellent students, it can never go anything but well, Father."

Father Herb turned to Viejo and introduced the twin girls, who appeared to be in their early teens. "This is Gracie," he said, "and this is Sonya. Sonya has a hearing impairment. She is learning to play by feeling the vibration of the various chords. Isn't that right, Sonya?"

Gracie signed to Sonya, and Sonya, smiling enthusiastically, nodded her head in the affirmative.

"We believe in offering diverse opportunities, enabling the kids to improve in many areas. Learning how to play music is one of them," Romero said. "None of their parents can afford to buy their kids a musical instrument, let alone pay for music lessons. We step in where the parents can't."

"We believe these skills help to build self-esteem," Father Herb added. "As well as substituting positive activities in place of undesirable activities."

"I've always enjoyed music. Wish I had learned to play when I was growing up," Viejo replied. He gave the girls a thumbs-up and turned to continue the tour.

"We're not trying to be noble, Jim," Father Herb said. "If what we do is noble, so be it. We're just trying to stick a finger in the dam of misery flowing freely around these parts. That's it. Nothing high and mighty. Just the basics. Best we can do, given our limited resources."

In the next classroom, a girl who looked to be about eighteen was working on a computer while wearing headphones. Father Herb leaned in and whispered, "This is Rachel Gomez. Been here about a year. Had to drop out of high school because she got pregnant. Another victim of the 'baby mama' trap."

"That's commonplace here," Romero said. "In fact, Albuquerque could be the poster child for the baby mama endemic prevalent in many inner-city neighborhoods throughout the nation. It's particularly bad here, though."

"You already met the father of the child . . . Roque Sanchez, the worst of the bunch, if you ask me," Father Herb said.

Viejo said nothing. Silently wishing he had punched the guy.

"Rachel is studying hard for her GED, and when she gets it, I've hooked her up with a job as a legal assistant," Romero said. "She's also taking an online course geared to working in a law office. All good stuff! I'm proud of her."

They left Rachel's study room and headed to the facility's cafeteria. It looked to Viejo like any average institutional dining area. He noticed every table was full as lunch was being served.

"We do more than teach and nurture the soul here," Father Herb said. "Without the breakfasts and lunches that we serve seven days a week, many of these kids would go hungry."

"Their worthless fathers never take responsibility for the kids they produce solely for proof of their own masculinity," Romero said, the disgust obvious in her voice. "The kids grow up without traditional family values, enabling the cycle to keep repeating itself."

As they walked to the front door, Father Herb and Romero asked what Viejo thought of the place.

"Looks like you're doing really good things here," Viejo said, "but I'm not sure if I'm the right man for the job. Not exactly a spring chicken myself. Not sure if I have enough gas left in the tank to do something like this. As Renee saw in her classroom and my encounter with Roque, I have a natural inclination to respond violently at times. It came in handy in combat, but not sure that makes me such a great role model."

"You don't have to decide right now, or anytime soon, for that matter. But will you think about it?" Romero asked.

"Thinking's not exactly my strong suit, but yeah, I'll think about it. Maybe this is a chance to wipe my slate clean."

"That's all I can ask for now," Father Herb said. "Think about it. Pray about it. If you feel the Lord is leading you to do this, let us know."

"I will," Viejo said. "And soon. I just have to be sure is all."

"We understand," Romero offered. "Now, let's get that lunch I promised you."

It was only a short drive over to Henry Apodaca's Famous Tacos Café. The noon crowd had dwindled by the time they arrived. There were several empty tables. They selected a two-seater near the rear window. Spotting them, Henry scurried over to their table.

"Hola, Judge Renee! Haven't seen you in a while. You want the usual?"

"Why wouldn't I? Can't go wrong with the world's best tacos . . . *mas major en todo el mundo!*"

Beaming from the compliment, Henry nodded in agreement. "I'd like to be modest, but yes, my tacos are undoubtedly the world's best." Looking at Viejo, he said, "And for you, sir?"

"Looks like I'd be a real idiot if I didn't order the same."

Henry hurried back to the kitchen.

"Okay, now that I've placed myself in your hands, just what did I order?"

"We are having the Taco Trio plate one each of fish, pork, and ground beef, along with sides of pinto beans and Spanish rice. If you don't absolutely love it, I'll have to assume you're either some kind of communist or your taste buds are dysfunctional."

Romero's cell phone buzzed. She glanced at the screen. "Sorry, I have to take this. It's my renter." She listened, nodding, and replied, "That'll be fine, Courtney. Don't worry about it. I can return your damage deposit tomorrow."

Turning to Viejo she said, "That was Courtney, the young lady who rents the casita behind my house. She just accepted a job offer in Washington and has to move out right away. If you want, I can show you the place this afternoon. I think it would be perfect for you."

"Guess I can cram another activity into my non-schedule."

12

Jim Viejo

PRESENT TIMES

OMERO TURNED OFF THE MAIN ROAD ONTO A secluded access lane that led into the heart of an exclusive wooded subdivision populated with custom-built homes on large, manicured lots.

"You live in here?" Viejo asked, incredulous.

Romero laughed. "Yes, I do. I told you I made a boatload of money in corporate law."

"I'll say. By appearances, it looks like the boat was about the size of an aircraft carrier."

She turned off the access road onto a single-lane paved driveway winding back through the trees. Stands of pine and deciduous trees hemmed the Lexus in on both sides. At the end of the lane, Romero pulled into a circular driveway in front of a large two-story territorial-style hacienda.

"Nice digs," Viejo commented.

"You can thank my ex-husband for that," Romero said, shutting down the car. "Besides coming from old money, he was, uh, *is* an extremely successful trial attorney, litigating on behalf of some of the biggest companies in the nation. When the divorce went through, he didn't have a leg to stand on because he clearly cheated on me with his assistant. He wanted to settle quickly and quietly to avoid embarrassment. Money was no object. I got the house as part of the settlement."

"Not a bad deal," Viejo said, opening the passenger side door and getting out.

Romero joined him.

"I'll show you around the main house later," Romero said. "First, let's go check out the guest casita. I think you'll like it."

Viejo thought he probably would, based on what he had seen thus far. He was happy to be staying with Mary Jane and the grandkids, but he also didn't want to disrupt the family dynamic. Guests, he knew, were like fish. They start to smell bad after a few days.

Romero motioned for him to follow her as she walked briskly around the front wraparound porch to a gravel path leading through a wooded, parklike area.

"This is my favorite part of the property. I like to sit out here and chill. Listen to the wind and the birds, feel the warm breeze on my skin. I've always loved nature. It gives me peace and brings me closer to God."

"It also brings you closer to the bugs."

Romero giggled. "You take the good with the bad."

Up ahead, Viejo saw the guest house. It was a beautiful territorial with a front porch, obviously designed to be a mini version of the hacienda.

"Man, it's gorgeous!" Viejo said, greatly impressed. "I'm not sure I can afford the rent on a colonel's retirement."

"Oh, don't worry about that. I've always rented it below market rate. I don't need the money, and I feel safer having someone out here."

"Uh-huh."

Romero unlocked the front door and stepped inside. Viejo followed her in. The entry foyer sported hardwood floors that glistened in the sunlight. Beyond was a cozy living room leading to an open dining area.

"This is beautiful!" Viejo said as she showed him around.

"Here's the master suite," she said, opening the door to a bedroom with large windows overlooking the forest behind her property. A lush Oriental carpet served as an area rug. The king-size bed featured a dark mahogany headboard. Expensive brass lamps sat on the two nightstands on either side of the bed.

"You sure didn't go cheap when you were furnishing this place," Viejo said. "It's done up for royalty."

"I wouldn't quite say that, but yeah, it is a bit upscale. That's the way my ex liked things. Nothing but the best for him. And, you know what? To a point, I think that's okay. Why shouldn't we get what we want in life if we work hard to get it, as long as we also remain generous with what we have?"

"It appears you've struck a good balance between rewarding yourself and helping others," Viejo said.

She led the way into a modern kitchen featuring a granite-topped island with matching granite counters. Dark cherry cabinets contrasted nicely with the stonework.

"I hope you like to cook," Romero said, shooting him a big smile. "This kitchen has everything you need. No need to purchase utensils or stuff like that."

"Glad to hear it. I traveled light. Got rid of most of my stuff at Camp Pendleton. I'm out for a new start, so I figured traveling with a lot of baggage didn't make much sense."

"I get it," Romero said. "Easier to dump the physical baggage than the emotional baggage, though."

"Not going to argue with that."

Viejo didn't have to think another second about whether he wanted to move into the guest house.

"I'll take it," Viejo said. "How soon can I move in?"

Romero smiled broadly. "I'm glad. It's a little isolated way out here. You can move in as soon as Courtney vacates. Probably in a couple of days. Looks like she's leaving it spotless, so I won't have to hire a cleaning service to get it ready."

"Perfect. It would be nice to spend a little more time with my family before I move in."

13

Jim Veijo

PRESENT TIMES

VIEJO GAZED OUT THE WINDOW OF THE GONDOLA AT the stunning views of the Sandia Mountains as it slowly climbed to the summit on the Sandia Peak Tramway.

Viejo glanced over at Father Herb, who seemed to be lost in thought. After settling in at Romero's casita, he'd spent several days in self-imposed isolation, trying to plot a strategy for moving forward. He'd told his daughter he needed some time alone and Romero had readily agreed to give him as much time alone as he needed.

The quiet time wasn't working as well as he had anticipated. After three days, his ducks still weren't lining up in order. He realized the futility of trying to resolve issues on his own. He needed help. Father Herb appeared to be the right man for the job. Although Viejo's faith was admittedly on shaky ground, there was something about the priest. Perhaps there was some sort of spiritual connection between Father Herb and himself? Was God finally done punishing him and had led him to the priest for the purpose of guiding him back from five years of misery?

Father Herb answered, sounding eager to take his call.

"I'm glad you want to get together, Jim," Father Herb responded. "I thought you might like to talk. I've been expecting your call."

"How did you know I was going to call?"

"That's a discussion for another time. For now, let's just focus on helping you help yourself. I think the perfect venue would be a walk in the mountains. I'll meet you tomorrow at the base of the tram. There are some great trails up there. Very peaceful. Perfect for reflection."

The tram arrived at the top, and soon the passengers disembarked, along with Viejo and Father Herb. Viejo followed Father Herb to one of the several hiking trails that spiraled off from the tram stop. They walked in silence for a while until they reached a remote scenic overlook.

"Boy, it's beautiful up here," Viejo said, looking down at the expanses of green forests, boulders, and vast stretches of bare gray rock on the steep slopes.

"It certainly is God's country. I wanted to take you up here to get closer to God, if that makes sense."

Viejo sighed. "I'm not sure there's a place for God in my life. Doesn't appear that He has a place for me either."

Father Herb looked straight ahead, apparently lost in thought.

Viejo continued. "I've been torn up inside for so long; I'm tired of fighting it. I know I can't move on until I can find some peace."

Father Herb sat quietly, saying nothing, only nodding and smiling at Viejo as an encouragement to continue.

"I was still reeling from the loss of Betti when my son, Michael, was killed in action about a year ago during the first days of the Iraq War. I was raised in a Christian family and had always been traditionally spiritual. The losses combined to make me challenge everything my parents and the Church had taught me about God, about love, about life . . . about everything. The only logical conclusion was that God was punishing me for my sins."

"What sins do you think you've committed?" Father Herb asked, his voice gentle, reproachless. "Take your time."

Viejo didn't need to take his time. He knew damn well that God was punishing him for all the men he'd killed in his time in the Corps, as well as for all the men he'd trained in the art of killing. He laid it out in no uncertain terms for Father Herb, becoming more remorseful and bitter as the confession escalated into a rant.

"I have enough blood on my hands to fill an Olympic-size swimming pool," Viejo concluded, barely able to choke out the words.

Father Herb moved over and put a hand on his shoulder. "It's okay, Jim, let it out. The tough guy façade has been part of the problem. Keeps things bottled up inside where they do the most damage."

"I didn't cry at Betti's funeral, and now I'm losing it up here on top of a mountain in front of a guy I barely know."

Waves of embarrassment, pain, and sadness washed over him like surf. All the emotions he'd been hiding erupted.

"I'm a killer," Viejo sobbed. "I deserve all the pain I have."

"No, you don't," Father Herb said.

"Yeah, I do. But why would a loving God take my wife and son to punish me? That's not the sort of God they taught me to love when I was a kid. What if God isn't done with me and will take whoever I love next, just to make a point that I'm a sinner and deserve to live in pain?"

"God is love, and love is God. You can't be afraid of love, and you shouldn't go forward believing that God's going to hurt others for the sake of punishing you. He doesn't work that way."

"Sure seems like it."

Father Herb got up from the bench and paced back and forth with his hands folded behind his back. He remained silent for a few long moments before he said, "Let me make something perfectly clear. None of us receive God's love and forgiveness because we deserve them. Even the best of us are closer to being like the vilest human who ever lived than we are similar to being like Christ. Forgiveness is purely and solely a function of grace—a grace won for us by Christ's sacrifice on the cross. It's a gift received through faith. I assume all those you killed were in combat situations?"

Viejo, regaining partial control, nodded grudgingly.

"And all the men killed by those you trained were also in combat.

Correct?"

"Yeah, that's right."

"The soldier who kills in combat is merely the weapon, not the killer. The commandment about not killing would probably be clearer if it said 'thou shalt not murder' instead of 'thou shalt not kill.' Do you think David sinned when he killed Goliath? Was it wrong to kill Nazis? No, it wasn't."

Father Herb sat back down next to Viejo. "Does any of this make sense to you?" he asked.

Suddenly, a thought crystallized in Viejo's mind. "You know," he said, "no one ever explained it to me like that. Are you telling me I've been running around spiritually flagellating myself because of semantics? Because I never made a distinction between killing and murder? Can it really be that simple? What I've done can't be forgivable. It can't be that easy. I don't know if I can buy this. I've been in a dark place for five long years, believing that God must hate me even more than I hate myself for what I've done in the past. It's the only explanation that makes sense. Why else would I lose both Betti and Michael?"

"God doesn't hate you. He created you. He doesn't hate anyone. He loves. I don't expect you to accept my answers on faith, nor do I suggest that your healing process isn't going to take time. But you have to begin, and to begin, you have to want to begin. The first step is to realize that your experience in combat wasn't wrong. Your self-loathing and guilt are self-imposed. God loves you and wants to lead you on the path to self-acceptance. He didn't punish your wife or Michael because of anything you did. He simply has a plan for them that neither of us understands. Sometimes, God presents us with situations that, given our human level of understanding, appear to be irresolvable paradoxes. That's why we have to rely on faith rather than on our limited intelligence."

They sat in silence. Viejo sighed, realizing that while he wanted to believe what the priest had told him, he had found some sort of pitiful refuge in his anger at God. It gave him a focal point, a way to avoid the tough job of healing. Along with help from his pills and alcohol, his anger was an easy way out of grief but maybe it was the opposite—an easy way into a life of self-imposed misery, an excuse for not trying to get better.

"I'm being punished by God, and there's nothing I can do about it." Accepting Father Herb's explanation and acting on it would take a huge effort. Was he up to it? Maybe God did love him and had led him to Father Herb because He was tired of watching him wallow in his self-pity and anger.

Viejo turned to Father Herb. "I realize I'm not in the express line to get into heaven, with twenty sins or less in my sin basket, but I can't go on like this, Father Herb. I just can't. One minute, I'm the life of the party, and the next, I want to kill myself. I may already be hooked on valium, and I don't want to go any farther down the chemical trail. I can't keep relying on drugs or booze to find the artificial peace they provide."

"That's the spirit!" Father Herb said, clapping his hands together. "You're taking an important step right now by acknowledging that you have a problem with pills, as well as with alcohol. If you face up to that and take steps to get off the pills and booze, you'll be better able to focus on more steps in the right direction.

"Use the psychological principle of substitution. Start doing things you feel good about, which will gradually replace the feelings of guilt with feelings of satisfaction about how you are living your life."

"Like volunteering at the clinic?"

"Guilty as charged! I was hoping I could find a way to work that into our conversation." Father Herb laughed. "You've lived an active life. I don't see how shifting into neutral and coasting across the finish line would work for a guy like you. Better to shift into a higher gear and accelerate to the finish!"

They hurried back up the trail and took the tram down just as a brilliant sunset was bathing the landscape, putting a cherry on top of the best day Viejo had experienced in a long time.

14

Betti

'M WATCHING JIM AS HE STANDS AT THE BATHROOM SINK, getting ready for bed. His hands are shaking. He's sweating, going through withdrawal from those damned pills. He splashes cold water on his face, leans forward, and grabs the edge of the sink, taking slow, deep breaths, trying to gain control over the physical reactions.

This is hard to watch. It pains me to see him this way, but I know he has to win this fight with addiction. Last week, during one of our regular one-sided bedtime conversations, Jim told me about his conversation on the mountain with Father Herb. He senses there is something special, something different about the old priest, a spiritual connection of sorts. Jim came away with a new perspective, along with a long overdue resolve to escape his darkness. An important part of the escape plan is to break free from the pills.

He splashes more cold water on his face and dries off with a towel. Hands still shaking, he opens the medicine cabinet.

"No! Don't do it!" I scream. Of course, he can't hear me.

He takes the bottle out of the cabinet and holds it close to his face as if to study the label.

"Okay, big guy," he whispers to himself, "I don't know if you can make it without these little amigos, but you gotta try."

I can scarcely believe what I'm hearing.

"Your grandkids think you're some kind of hero," he says, putting the bottle on the counter next to the sink. "What would they think of you if they knew the truth? That you're a miserable pill-popping weakling who can't get through the day without a medicinal crutch?"

I think I know the answer to that. They'd be terribly disappointed in him, just as I have been. I have been hoping and praying for five long years that he'd crawl his way out of the deep hole he dug for himself after my death. With Michael's death, the hole got deeper and the sides steeper. Clearly, he's at a crossroads, a choice that will determine the trajectory of his life. Has Father Herb guided him toward the right choice?

I watch with great suspense as he picks up the bottle again. He takes the cap off and pours a handful of pills into the palm of his left hand. He pinches one between his right thumb and index finger, brings it to his lips.

Do . . . not . . . do . . . it!

"Adios, amigo!" he says, his voice suddenly strong.

I feel overjoyed when I see him go to the toilet and drop the tablet into the bowl. In it goes with a tiny plop!

"We aren't amigos anymore!" he shouts and empties the rest of the bottle into the toilet.

I smile as I watch him raise both hands above his head, the empty bottle still clutched in his right fist.

Quietly, he says, "Jesus, please give me the strength to do this. I can't do it alone. Not without your help. Not without your love."

I realize he's suddenly not hating God any longer. He's not feeling like God is punishing him, or at least possibly he's not feeling that as strongly as he did before. I know it's going to take him some time to fully heal and that the process is going to be slow and painful, but I get the feeling that my tough old Marine is on his way. I'm delighted. With faith and support from the people around him, Jim will find his way back into the light. He'll leave the darkness in his wake and never look back. I can only hope, observe, and give him the feeling of my presence, just as I am now.

Jim lowers his arms, opens the door under the sink cabinet, and tosses the empty bottle into the trash can. He closes the door and stares at himself in the mirror for a long moment.

"Betti?" he asks. "Is that you? You there, Betti? I can feel you. It's almost like you're standing right here!"

I'm right here! I'm not standing, Jim, but I'm right here with you. I'm rooting for you, Jim! I want you to find the happiness you deserve!

He runs his hands over his buzz-cut hair, shakes his head and looks down at his trembling hands.

"Maybe I should've kept just a couple," he says, then shakes his head, "No, it doesn't work like that, right, Betti? Gotta quit cold turkey. Gotta be strong! Gotta open up a big old can of Marine-style whip-ass!"

I want to scream that he's right, that what he's setting out to do won't be easy, but he can do it. He walks out of the bathroom and moves to the nightstand, picks my music box up and examines it with a curious look on his face. I know he can feel my presence, especially at the moment. He appears to be drawing upon the strength I am radiating. I want him to get stronger so he can find happiness in just being alive and rejoicing in the love of other people. I want him to find romantic love again. Will it be with Renee? It could happen, and that makes me happy for both of them.

"I know you love me. I know you feel my love in return," he says softly. "What we have doesn't die."

I'll always love you, Jim . . . even after you set me free.

15

Jim Viejo

PRESENT TIMES

A TYPICALLY STUNNING NEW MEXICO SUNSET dominated the Western sky. Viejo and Romero were enjoying a glass of better-than-average cabernet on the front porch of the casita. Over the past few weeks, he had been slowly adjusting to the slower pace of life as a retiree, filling his time with excursions with the grandsons and helping Peyton install a large deck to the rear of their home. Early mornings were spent in long, meditative walks through the wooded neighborhood, using them as an opportunity to digest the spiritual vitamins provided by Father Herb. He wasn't completely sold, but the more he thought about the priest's viewpoints, the more they made sense. He was beginning to heal. He had not refilled the prescription for his pills. Drinking was confined to an occasional shared bottle of wine with Renee.

Looking at her as she sipped her wine, he realized how much he had missed over the past five years, during his self-imposed numbness to feelings. Which was the more honorable option? Honoring his wedding vow to Betti that he would love only her forever, or honoring her last request that he find happiness with another woman? Clearly, the second option was Betti's choice. Shouldn't her choice trump his? He guessed, hoped, actually, that Renee wanted to take their relationship to a higher level, but he was unsure how to play his part. He'd had zero courting experience since he met Betti. *It's a pretty good bet*, he thought, *that what a woman expected from a relationship over twenty years ago wouldn't be the same as now.* Besides, she was still seeing Howard, although it was easy to see her heart wasn't in it. He didn't want to do something clumsy and ruin his chances. What if he would never going heal completely? If so, Renee would be better off without him in her life. It would be unfair to start something that would eventually drag her down with him.

Viejo snapped back to the present, realizing they had both been lost in thought. Neither had said a word for a good fifteen minutes.

"Penny for your thoughts," he ventured.

"In view of inflation. I'll probably have to charge you at least a nickel. But, since you asked, I've been thinking that you are obviously going to be bored to death if you don't find something positive to do. I hope you are getting close to a decision about volunteering at the clinic, but I'm not going to bug you about it tonight. Instead, I'm going to spice up your life by inviting you to go on a balloon ride with me tomorrow morning. It took longer than expected, but the new burners have finally been installed, and I can't wait to fly again. Are you up for it?"

"Up for it? Clever pun. I hope my life insurance covers this sort of thing. Sure, I'd love to try it!"

"Don't worry. Statistically, it's safer than riding a bicycle on a busy street."

16

Jim Viejo
PRESENT TIMES

VIEJO STOOD IN A FIELD ON THE NORTHERN OUTSKIRTS of the city with Romero, Father Herb, and the flight crew, ready for the aerial adventure. His eyes widened as he looked at the overgrown wicker basket, the aluminum burner, and most impressively, the envelope, which Romero explained to him was balloon-speak for the actual balloon, a sixty-foot elongated bag. She told him the envelope was constructed of material similar to that used for parachutes.

"Speaking of parachutes," he began.

"We don't use them," she answered, smiling mischievously at Viejo's look of concern.

"No parachutes? Are you sure this thing's safe?"

"Yeah, real safe. I take it up all the time."

Despite his reservations, the prospect of flying in a balloon excited him. He'd never gone up in one, but he suspected from the research he had done last night it was a sort of rite of passage for being an Albuquerquean. The city billed itself as the "hot-air ballooning capital of the world." The weather conditions, typically dry and cool, were highly conducive to ballooning for much of the year, attracting more resident balloon owners than any other city on the planet. More than three-hundred residents owned and flew balloons on a regular basis, and, of course, most of them participated in the Albuquerque International Balloon Fiesta, a nine-day balloon blast held every October, routinely hosting over five hundred pilots and attracting spectators by the tens of thousands. He planned to live the rest of his life in Albuquerque. It would be embarrassing to admit he had never been up in a balloon.

He clearly saw how much Romero loved the sport as she directed the crew to lay the long envelope out on the ground. Ties at intervals kept it from losing shape in the gentle breeze. The three men in the crew attached the bottom edge of the balloon to the basket and frame, and then the crew leader, Elliott, who co-owned the balloon with Renee, fired up a giant gas-powered fan to blow cold air into the balloon to begin the inflation process.

"This is what we call the cold inflation stage," Romero said, turning to him with a big smile on her face.

"Cold what?" Viejo asked, genuinely curious, reveling in the new experience.

"Cold inflation. First, you have to get air inside the envelope to puff the fabric out. See?" she asked, pointing toward the rainbow-patterned envelope. "Like that. See how it's billowing out now?"

Viejo nodded. Billow, it did. It looked like the thing was breathing. The fabric rose and fell and moved from side to side like a giant creature coming to life.

"Okay, now watch what Elliott does next!" she said.

Raul walked over to the burners and fired them up. Blue flames sprouted from the tops of the two burners, one a main burner and the other a backup. The flames turned orangish yellow as the three-foot jets of heat spewed into the now gaping mouth of the balloon.

"That's called hot inflation," Romero said. "We shoot heated air into the balloon to inflate it."

"Looks kinda dangerous."

Romero playfully punched his left arm. "Hot air is less dense than cold air. You know that heat rises, right?"

"Yeah, everyone knows that."

"Well, heating the air inside the balloon makes the air inside lighter than the air outside the balloon, which causes lift. See!" she gushed. "See how it's becoming upright!"

The balloon slowly rose. He stared at it, transfixed, as the rainbow design decorating the balloon became more apparent. The balloon rose from the ground, becoming fully inflated.

"This a standard size for a balloon?"

Romero nodded.

"Yes, it is. Sixty feet is pretty much the norm. When she's fully inflated, the envelope contains 77,000 cubic feet of hot air. There are bigger balloons, but they are much more expensive, and they require a bigger flight crew. This size is just fine for Elliott and me. You really gotta love it! Isn't she beautiful?"

Viejo said he agreed. The rainbow balloon was emblazoned with "Both Sides of the Rainbow" on each side in bright gold letters. He immediately thought of Betti and fought back the wave of powerful emotions suddenly bubbling to the surface. He swallowed hard. Clenched his fists.

"Something wrong, Jim?" Romero asked, surprised at his unexpected reaction.

Taking a deep breath and exhaling loudly, Viejo said, "'Somewhere Over the Rainbow' was our favorite song. Betti and me. We used to love it. You know, I keep her ashes in a special music box that plays the song whenever I wind it up. It was her idea. She asked me to play it whenever I needed strength."

Viejo choked up. Romero stepped close and gave him a gentle hug.

"I'm so sorry to trigger the sad memories. I know you loved her very much." Tearing up herself, she added, "That's probably the most heartfelt, romantic thing I've ever heard. She was a lucky woman."

"I was the lucky one."

Despite his emotions, Viejo noticed that his comment didn't seem to bother Romero. She didn't appear jealous at all. Just the opposite. She admired his devotion to his late wife.

The balloon stood tall, towering its full sixty feet above them. Viejo was amazed at the fifty-five-foot width of the envelope. The sheer size of the thing made for an awesome sight. Seemingly anxious to be free, it tugged on the anchor lines attached to the basket. Viejo looked over at Father Herb, who stood a distance away, possibly to give them privacy or perhaps offer prayers for a safe flight. Noticing his look, Father Herb smiled and walked over to them.

"Looks like we're about ready for the test flight," Elliott said. "The new burners appear to be working just fine."

"Seems so," Romero said. "They better. They cost a mint."

"Worth every penny, I'm sure," Father Herb said. Turning to Viejo, he asked, "You ready for this adventure? I am certain it will be memorable!"

"Not sure about that, but I'm up for some fun flying. Never been up in a hot-air balloon before."

"It's heavenly," Father Herb said. "And you'll love the end part. You'll see."

Viejo didn't like the sound of that.

"What about the end part?" he asked.

Father Herb just grinned as if he knew something nobody else did.

"When the chase truck picks us up," Romero volunteered.

"Chase truck?"

"Yeah, chase truck," Romero replied. "You know, you can't steer a balloon. Balloons ride the wind. They go where the wind goes, and you've got to go with them. It's a lot like life in that respect. You go with the flow because you've got no other choice."

"Chase truck?" Viejo repeated. "You sure this thing is safe? Seems to me that if it was safe, you would have a meet-us-at-the-designated-landing-spot-truck instead of a chase truck."

"Like I said, you can't steer a balloon, so Elliott will follow us in his pickup. Oh, Elliott, I almost forgot. Did you put the bottle of champagne in the basket?"

"I will never forget the most important part, *mi amiga*."

"Bottle of champagne?" Viejo asked, definitely puzzled. "Aren't there laws against drunken balloon flying? You know, getting high while you're getting high? Something like that?"

Romero laughed. "It's not to drink. Balloon tradition calls for a champagne dousing after your first balloon flight. Breaking the tradition would bring you a lifetime of bad luck."

"Okay, then. I guess a champagne shower beats a lifetime of bad luck."

Father Herb laughed. "It certainly does. I would have to schedule you for a confession if you didn't comply with this time-honored tradition, my son!"

"Well, boys," Romero said, putting both hands on her hips, "you ready to go up?"

Viejo warily eyed the three-foot-tall basket.

"That thing looks kinda small, now that I'm comparing it to the balloon," he said, pointing at the basket. "Looks like we could fall out pretty easily."

"You could if you were crazy enough to fool around up there. You crazy, Jim?"

"Probably crazier than you think!" he said.

"Seriously," Romero said. "It's safe. The only real danger is any power lines, and there aren't any out here. That and high winds. You can't land safely when it's really gusting. That's why we always check the weather forecast before we schedule a flight."

"Let's do this! I'll get in first, so you can give me a foot lift," Father Herb said, grabbing the edge of the basket.

Romero got in, and Viejo followed. He gripped one of the aluminum struts on the frame while the flight crew released the anchor lines. The balloon immediately began to ascend. The sensation was unlike anything Viejo had ever experienced. There was a feeling of quiet, gentle power as the balloon continued to ascend.

"This is amazing!" Viejo said, feeling a surge of adrenaline.

"You're getting closer to God every second," Father Herb said as he slapped Viejo gently on the back.

Romero pointed out the avionics. Viejo leaned toward the instrument panel as Romero explained the various gauges.

"This instrument is the altimeter. It shows how high we are."

"How high do you go up?" Viejo asked, genuinely curious and feeling a little more at ease.

"Typically, we fly no higher than three thousand feet. That way, we stay clear of civilian air traffic."

She paused and then explained that the instrument next to the altimeter was a rate-of-climb indicator to let her know how fast they were rising, plus an ambient air gauge to show atmospheric temperature outside the envelope.

She reached over and grabbed the mic of the ultra-high frequency citizen's band radio.

"Rainbow, Rainbow, Rainbow, do you copy Chase 1?" she asked.

She turned to Viejo and told him not to be alarmed; she was just testing the radio.

"Want to make sure it works," she laughed. "Don't worry about the static; it's typical until we get a little higher."

A moment later, the static stopped, and Elliott's voice came through loud and clear.

"That's a copy, Rainbow. Reading you loud and clear. Over."

"Roger that, Chase 1. Rainbow out."

They fell silent as the balloon continued to climb, expanding the exquisite view of the Sandia Mountains rising more than ten thousand feet to the east. Viejo knew that Spanish settlers named them "The Sandias", the Spanish word for watermelons. When the sun is shining brightly at sunset, the mountains reflect a beautiful red color. The tram running to the peak was clearly visible. To the west was the Rio Grande, winding amid fields of various row crops, alfalfa, and pastures. The fields created a checkered pattern, making the valley appear like a giant multi-patched quilt. Further west, the valley sloped up to form the West Mesa, with its five small dormant volcanoes, vestiges of past eons when the world looked much different.

"Everything looks so small from up here," Viejo said to no one in particular.

"The natural beauty up here always inspires, makes everything seem small, especially my problems," Romero offered.

"Nature is God. God is nature. God is the world," Father Herb interjected.

Romero fired the primary burner, giving the balloon more lift. She turned to Viejo and told him there was a sensor mounted at the top of the deflation vent at the peak of the balloon to indicate how hot it was inside the envelope.

"You never want it to get to over 248 degrees up there, or there could be big trouble," Romero said. "Big trouble."

Viejo was shocked. He had no idea how hot it got inside a hot-air balloon, but 248 degrees sounded like an inferno was raging inside the thin layer of fabric, keeping them aloft.

"Hope the sensor's working," Viejo said.

"Oh, it's working all right."

"Glad to hear it," Father Herb said.

They enjoyed the views in companionable silence. The experience was magical, producing a comfortable state of euphoria.

Breaking the silence, Viejo thanked Father Herb for their conversation on the mountaintop.

"You gave me some new ways to think about how I've lived my life and how I should live it in the future. I'm not sure if I really can or how long it might take, but I know I have to try. I know it's what Betti would want."

"She only wants you to be happy. She has ascended to a higher spiritual level, where jealousy doesn't exist, only love," Father Herb replied. "God's plan for her was just different from His plan for you. And he does have a plan for you, Jim. You just don't know what it is yet, but I promise, it's a good one."

"Remember to keep 1st Corinthians in mind as you work through your issues," Father Herb said. "'First, we see as through a mirror dimly.'"

"Have you given any more thought to the idea of volunteering at the clinic?" Romero asked. "I, uh, we really need you. You could do a lot of good there, especially for the boys."

"I have been thinking about it. A lot. And I'm leaning toward doing it. Just need to work a few more things out in my head. If I commit to this, I have to be in whole hog. I need to be really confident that I'll be the right guy in the right place at the right time."

"You know, waiting for everything to be perfect is an excuse for inaction," Father Herb said. "We can always find reasons not to do something. It's a lot harder to find reasons to do something, and it's even harder when something is unfamiliar. There is no downside to you being at the clinic. If it works out, your inner rewards would likely be just the therapy you need. If it doesn't work out, you can walk away and try something else."

Suddenly, they heard a tearing sound. Looking up inside the mouth of the balloon, it horrified them to see daylight through a rip at the top of the envelope. The balloon immediately began to lose altitude.

"Oh, my God!" Romero screamed. "That's not supposed to ever happen!"

"We gonna crash?" Viejo shouted, fear rising in his throat. He looked over at Father Herb, who didn't appear to be fazed at all.

Romero grabbed the mic of the CB. "Mayday! Mayday! Mayday! Hot-air balloon in distress over Thompson Road. Over."

The CB crackled. Elliott's panicked voice came through.

"Rainbow, Rainbow, Rainbow. This is Chase 1. What's happening up there?"

"We have a major tear near the deflation vent. We're losing altitude fast."

"We got your six, Rainbow. Chase 1 is standing by to assist."

"Roger that," Romero said. "I'm burning heat to slow our descent. I'm not sure how long I can keep her airborne. Rainbow out."

Viejo could tell she was scared out of her mind but managing to keep her cool. She fired the burner, giving it all the heat it could put out. The balloon continued to descend. Viejo was now certain they were going to crash. He felt totally helpless.

"I'm trying to ramp the heat up to slow our descent," Romero shouted over the roar of the burner. "But the heat's escaping out the top faster than I can replace it!"

Viejo watched in horror as the ground raced toward them. The breeze carried them steadily toward a lone Catholic Church, located just past a small cluster of adobe homes, which were appearing bigger by the second as the balloon's rate of descent increased. Viejo looked up and saw, again to his horror, that the envelope looked misshapen and flaccid.

We're in for it now! he thought. *I'm coming to you sooner than I thought, Betti!*

He looked over at Father Herb. The priest was smiling.

"Brace for impact!" Romero shouted, still firing the burner in a desperate attempt to slow their descent. "Everybody, fetal position on the floor!"

Viejo didn't need to be asked twice. Just as he was stooping to huddle inside the basket with his companions, he saw the church rushing toward them, and, for a moment, the irony of dying by crashing into a church aboard a distressed hot-air balloon was not lost on him. Could this be God's final, symbolic blow, a final repayment for his sins?

He felt the impact as the basket careened off the roof of the church and slid rapidly downward until it went over the edge and plummeted straight toward the ground. Romero screamed, and Viejo grit his teeth, hoping his death would be quick.

The basket suddenly stopped falling. It bobbed up and down, like an oversized yo-yo, several times and then began swinging gently back and forth.

"What just happened?" he asked, getting back on his feet and looking upward.

His companions stood up as well and looked up to see the top of the envelope snagged on the large cross atop the church spire. The basket continued to swing, suspended several feet above the ground.

"Well, would you look at that!" Father Herb exclaimed, trying to appear surprised by the miracle.

"Oh, my God! We're not dead!" Romero shouted, almost sobbing with joy. "God saved us!"

Father Herb turned to Viejo and said, "If you ever needed a sign that God isn't done with you yet, you just got a big one."

Viejo nodded in agreement. Assuming the role of an unflappable combat veteran, he asked, "Do I still get my champagne bath?"

Shaking from fear and adrenaline, Romero opened the bottle of champagne. She poured a small amount of champagne onto her fingertips and flicked it toward Viejo, wetting his face slightly.

"That's all you get for now," she said. "At the moment, I can think of a better use for the rest of this bottle!"

She took a big swig from the bottle and handed it to Viejo. He took a long pull and handed the bottle to Father Herb, who indulged as well. They climbed out of the basket and continued passing the bottle around as Elliott arrived in the chase truck and sprinted toward them.

"Everyone okay?" he asked.

"No harm, no foul," Viejo replied, attempting to appear unfazed. "But that was a little more exciting than I expected."

Romero laughed, the champagne beginning to take effect. "I may need a new pair of pants! It's a miracle we didn't get hurt or worse," she said.

"Yes," Father Herb ventured. "Perhaps a sign as well?"

Fire trucks, ambulances, and police cars arrived in a hurry. A large crowd from the neighborhood stood gaping at the bizarre scene of the balloon hanging from the spire. The local parish priest took numerous pictures and told Father Herb he was going to petition the Vatican to have the spot designated as a Holy Pilgrimage Site.

It took several hours to clean up the mess, answer questions from the various authorities involved, and conduct interviews with the local news media.

17

Renee Romero & Jim Viejo
PRESENT TIMES

ROMERO WAS FEELING A LITTLE TIPSY FROM THE champagne. Viejo drove them back to her house, where they went their separate ways to shower and catch some rest. Shortly after dusk, Viejo decided to see how she was doing. Armed with a bottle of wine, he walked down the lane through the backyard and knocked on her kitchen door.

She beamed at him as she opened the door.

"Hey, Jim!" Noting the wine, she said, "I see you came prepared."

Viejo laughed, holding the wine bottle up as if it was a grand prize.

"Yeah, I figured after the day we just had, we deserve a little extra libation."

"You're absolutely right about that. Come in," she said, holding the door open.

Standing near the kitchen sink, she took two wine glasses down from the cabinet over the counter and opened the wine with a corkscrew, pulling the cork with a satisfying pop.

"I hope the wine isn't too far below your standards," Viejo said. "Sophisticated people like you have wine collections. I merely have a wine supply. Most of which is only a tick above the kind you can buy in a box."

"Difference duly noted. At this point, I think I could drink kerosene."

Romero filled the wine glasses, set them on the kitchen table, and sat down across from Viejo.

As he looked at her, he felt a warm glow from within, a feeling he hadn't experienced in a long time. It wasn't surprising, but it was still a little disconcerting.

Romero held up her glass. "Cheers," she said and clinked glasses with him.

"Cheers."

They sipped the wine, watching Romero's corgi wolf down the lovely dinner she had prepared for him. They had often joked about the dog's gourmet diet. She readily admitted that she was way too obsessed, realizing that Georgie was a substitute for the children she had always wanted, but never had.

"Lucky dog," Viejo said, setting his wineglass back down on the table. "Eats better than the king of a small country. What's he getting tonight? Filet mignon?"

"No, just braised beef tips, but without the wine sauce. Poor dog."

"No wine sauce? They should report you to the ASPCA for animal cruelty."

Romero laughed as she ran her hands through her hair.

"I know I treat Georgie like a king. Can't help it. He's been my best friend for years."

"Isn't that a little sad?" Viejo asked.

Romero looked hurt. She said nothing for a long moment, then sighed and said she agreed.

"I've just been stuck lately," she said. "Stuck for a long time, really. Socially and career-wise. I'm hoping the changes I've made will help me find a new path forward."

"Speaking of the clinic," Viejo said, taking another sip of his wine and getting up from the table. He walked to the kitchen window and looked out into the dimly lit backyard. She had security lighting set up at intervals with motion detectors. With no movement outside, the lights were off. Only the back porch light illuminated a small area of the yard.

"I've decided to become a full-time volunteer at the clinic."

Romero clapped her hands and jumped up from the table, giving him a bear hug, which felt pretty good. He stepped back from her, his hands on her shoulders. He felt her warm breath, scented with the red wine, on his cheeks. Feeling awkward and afraid of making a huge mistake, he released her. Awkward and a little embarrassed, they sat back down.

"Been spending a lot of time thinking about the counseling I got from Father Herb. Everything he told me made perfect sense. Most of it was pretty simple. Made me realize I had put myself on a path to remain miserable instead of on a path toward healing. It seemed natural for me to assume that I was at fault. I've been putting off a decision to find a better path. Seems reasonable to take our balloon miracle as some sort of sign from God, just like Father Herb suggested. All of us would've been more comfortable with a more subtle sign on God's part, but I guess He thought that sometimes you have to hit a mule on the head with a two-by-four to get his attention. There's a good chance that I might need the clinic more than the clinic needs me. I read about a study where they looked at engineers who retired from a big company. The ones who didn't find something else to do died between three to five years after retiring. The ones who were more active lived considerably longer. Maybe working at the clinic will give me a reason to hang around a little longer."

Romero nodded, her face serious, but only for a moment. Then she grinned and said, "Maybe we can make you a he-man nametag."

"That would be funny," Viejo said. "A real stereotype for a retired Marine."

"Seriously, I'm so glad you decided to join our team," Romero said, reaching across the table and giving his right hand a quick squeeze, then withdrawing her hand. "I'm sure Father Herb will be thrilled. Jessie, as well."

Viejo felt a sense of satisfaction combined with relief at having made his decision about the clinic. He wasn't completely convinced he was ready. Father Herb's remark about waiting for things to be perfect, merely being a self-serving excuse, resonated with him. There would always be a reason not to act.

"I'm sure they will be. What's not to like about having another volunteer on deck?" Viejo said.

"Exactly."

Viejo enjoyed chatting with Romero as the evening progressed. They didn't talk about anything heavy except when the balloon crash came up several times. When the wine bottle was empty, he said goodnight and walked back to the guest house, triggering the security lights as he went.

He unlocked the front door of the guest house and stepped inside, flipping the light on as he closed the door behind him. He stood for a long moment, reflecting upon how such a nearly disastrous day had turned into such a pleasant evening. Where was all this heading? After preparing for bed, he stood in front of Betti's music box, strongly aware of her presence.

He stepped over to the dresser, wound up the music box, and set it back down as "Somewhere Over the Rainbow" played softly in the darkened room.

"Betti, I'm so confused. This feels so right and feels so wrong at the same time. You were and are the best part of my life. I owe you so much. I probably didn't tell you often enough. Didn't give you credit for the wonderful job you did with the kids. Thank God they turned out more like you than me. Now, this new deployment. I would like to think I'm doing this because it's the right thing to do . . . that God is leading me to do it. But maybe it's because of her. Is God leading me to the clinic? Or is He leading me to her? Or maybe both. Should I embrace these new changes in my life, or should I retreat before I wind up doing some damage?"

The music stopped playing. Viejo got into bed and turned off the lamp. He did not fall asleep right away. Instead, he replayed the balloon crash in his mind over and over again. The last thing on his mind before he drifted off was Romero. He kept seeing her deep green eyes, her beautiful smile, and hearing her utter the words, "I, uh, we need you."

He reminded himself that he had promised to help Peyton finish a small home improvement project tomorrow afternoon and then stick around for dinner. It would be a good idea to break the news about him joining the clinic that evening while everyone was together. Relaxing, he gradually drifted off into the best night's sleep he had enjoyed in years.

* * *

"Dinner's ready. Come and get it!" Mary Jane shouted through the kitchen window.

The timing was perfect. Peyton had just nailed the final floor plank into the deck frame. Viejo and the twins had been helping him all afternoon. Not that Peyton needed much help. He had grown up in his father's construction company, starting as a carpenter and progressing to be the company's project manager. When his father retired, Peyton and Mary Jane took over the business and soon built a strong reputation for building quality homes at reasonable prices. They typically had a long waiting list of customers eager to have them start their new homes.

After the family was seated and grace was offered, Viejo tapped on his glass to get their attention.

"I have an announcement. Starting next week, I am going to be a full-time volunteer at Father Herb's clinic. As you know, Renee and Father Herb have been trying to talk me into this since the day I arrived. I have taken the balloon incident as a sign that God has joined them in their efforts to recruit me. You'll probably be seeing a little less of me as I adjust to my new schedule."

"That's great news, Dad!" Mary Jane gushed. "What can we do to help you at the clinic?"

"I'm afraid that's a bit of a problem. There is a considerable amount of trouble with local gangs who want to shut down the clinic. There may be some violence. I don't want anyone about the clinic to know I have family in the area. There could be efforts at retaliation. I don't want to involve any of you until I know it is safe."

"I never considered there would be danger," Mary Jane responded. "Are you sure about this? We don't want anything to happen to you."

"Don't worry. This old Marine can take care of himself. It's the gangbangers who should be worried!"

18

Jim Viejo
PRESENT TIMES

T HE DAYS AND WEEKS PASSED QUICKLY AND ENJOYABLY for Viejo. He established a routine at the clinic, tutoring kids in math and overseeing study groups, along with his favorite activity, leading the physical education classes. Teaching physical activities came naturally to him. Very few of the older boys and girls who came to the clinic after school had ever participated in sports. They didn't have role model fathers who had enough interest in their development to introduce them to sports or any other positive activities, either at their schools or in city recreational programs. Most were being raised by single mothers who were the previous generation's equivalents of baby mamas. The cycle would be self-perpetuating if the gangs had their way.

He stood in front of his latest class on an early June morning; the kids lined up in orderly rows on the playing field. As public schools were no longer in session, the clinic was busier than ever.

Several of the teenagers had been convicted of minor offenses and had agreed to attend the clinic for the summer in exchange for a lighter punishment from the courts. The more ambitious ones needed the math tutoring to retake classes they had flunked. It was not surprising that they struggled in the classroom, given the lack of resources and support they experienced at home. Viejo was determined to make a difference with those who were just killing time, waiting to turn old enough to drop out of school. New Mexico allowed teens as young as sixteen to drop out of school with proof of hardship. Most of the baby-mama-raised kids could prove hardship. Their parents didn't care about education and would file the paperwork. The sperm-donor dads would just as soon get them out of school and into the gangs as soon as possible.

There were about twenty teenage boys dressed in typical, sloppy, low-hanging shorts and torn T-shirts. Interestingly, many of the kids wore expensive sneakers.

"Okay, rookies! Drop and gimme twenty!" Viejo shouted, pacing back and forth in front of the class, doing his perfect drill sergeant imitation.

None of the kids so much as budged.

"What's the matter? You can't do twenty pushups? You guys that out of shape?"

"We don't do pushups, man," one of the kids said. "Dunno why I'm even standing here wasting my time."

Viejo walked over to the kid and got in his face like a drill sergeant.

"You're here because your mother is inside studying for her GED, and she doesn't want you out on the street getting into all kinds of trouble. You get me, Louis? You understand me now?"

Viejo noted the look of disgust on Louis's face, but he also saw a flash of respect. The kids knew he was an ex-Marine with extensive combat experience. Word got around fast, or so he was told, that it wasn't a good idea to provoke the new guy at the clinic, which was just fine with Viejo. He welcomed the reputation of being someone nobody should mess with. One of the few things that earned "street cred" was physical toughness. Viejo had it and knew how to project it. The gangbangers had abandoned their gauntlet at the front gate after he offered to fight the two biggest ones at the same time. If they won, he'd leave them alone; if he won, they'd back off. It didn't take long for them to show their true colors and scatter like cockroaches.

Louis nodded. "Yeah, I get you."

"Well, then," Viejo said, stepping back in front of the group, "let this old man show you how it's done!" He dropped and quickly did fifty pushups, hardly breathing hard in the effort. "Your turn! Gimme twenty!"

Not wanting to be shown up by an "old man", the kids attempted to comply. He watched as they huffed and puffed. None could do more than a few reps. They were embarrassed; their weakness exposed. It was hard for them to maintain their tough-guy personas in this scenario. This was exactly what Viejo wanted. His plan was to give them a goal to work toward. He told them it was okay if they couldn't do twenty pushups today.

"Today's lesson just provided a starting point. The ability to set goals and formulate plans for accomplishing them is a key factor in creating a successful life. The process involves identifying a starting point and then creating intermediate steps leading toward accomplishing the ultimate goal. Our twenty-push-up goal is a great way to learn the process because it is simple and measurable. Okay, let's assume that your starting point is four pushups. I want you to practice at home, and each Friday, we will test again. Your intermediate goal will be to increase your pushups by three pushups per week. At that rate, in about five weeks, you should be able to do twenty. When *everyone* in the class can do twenty, I'll arrange for a special lunch at the cafeteria to celebrate. The 'everyone' component to this exercise is to give you a lesson in teamwork. You will experience the benefit of encouraging others in the group as well as the pressure of not wanting to let the group down."

The following week, every kid in the class could do at least seven pushups. As the weeks progressed, with the intermediate goals being achieved as planned, Viejo could see a sense of pride growing in the class. He lavished praise and encouragement on them. They were from an environment consisting of low expectations. This was new territory for them. They had never been taught how to set a goal, plan how to make it happen, and look forward to a reward when the goal was accomplished.

At the end of five weeks, every kid could do at least twenty pushups. Viejo scheduled the promised special lunch, honoring the kid's request for green chili cheeseburgers and ice cream, paying for it out of his own pocket. Gazing around the room, it amazed him how this simple process had been so transitional for the class in such a short time. Five weeks ago, they were a sullen group, barely bothering to communicate with each other. Now, they were busy chatting away, embedded in newly formed friendships arising from their shared positive experience.

Louis raised his hand to get Viejo's attention.

"Mr. Viejo . . . what's next? Five more weeks to get to forty pushups?"

"Great question, Louis! I think you are about to discover that success breeds success. This process is intended to get you to start to think of goals and how to accomplish them. There's nothing wrong with establishing another pushup goal, but I want you to look beyond that. You have your entire lives ahead of you, the great majority of which will be spent as adults. I want you to dream a little. What do you want to do with your life? What do you want to be? The goal setting and planning process for something as simple as our pushup project is the basic process for achieving your dreams. You define your goal, assess where you are now in relation to your goal, and form a plan to get from where you are to where you want to be. I realize you guys don't have the backing and resources that wealthy families can offer their kids, but this is America. You can still make it happen. You just have to work harder and smarter than the privileged kids. A piece of advice: the first step to create opportunities for yourselves is to do well in school. Our public education systems offer a world of knowledge. Start soaking it up! I'm around here most days. Tell me what your dream is, and I'll help you identify the steps to get there. The rest is up to you."

19

Jim Viejo
PRESENT TIMES

SUMMER WAS RUSHING BY. VIEJO WAS CONDUCTING his final math tutoring session. The students had made excellent progress, and he felt confident they would pass their algebra class this time around.

Suddenly, the door to the classroom burst open, and Jessie ran into the room, out of breath and almost tripping, as she caught herself on his desk.

"Jim! Jim! You gotta get outside right now!" she said, the panic in her voice setting off alarm bells in Viejo's head. "Roque just punched Rachel in the face!"

"He did what?"

"He hit her! Now he's out there yelling at her to move back in with him and start hooking again. Worse yet, he's got his father with him," Jessie said, breaking down in tears. "I never thought I'd see that monster again! He should still be in prison!"

"Come on, let's go!" he said, getting up and running with her through the clinic out to the front entrance.

He saw Rachel hunched over, sobbing uncontrollably. Her daughter, Isabella, clutched her right leg and looked away from Roque, who was standing close to Rachel as he cursed her. Viejo, instantly enraged, grabbed Roque's right arm and pulled him away from the young mother and her toddler. He spun him around to face him, reared back, and gut-punched him. Hard. Roque doubled over, wheezing, the wind knocked out of him.

"If I ever see you hit this woman, or anyone else for that matter, I'm going to beat you so bad you'll be sucking your food through a straw for the rest of your sorry life!"

Roque got his wind back and stood up straight, both hands clenched in fists, ready to strike.

"Don't even think about it," Viejo said, his voice a low, menacing growl. "Not if you know what's good for you."

"I'm gonna kill you for that."

"You're welcome to try, but I don't like your odds. I could whip a platoon of punks like you without breaking a sweat. Now, get the hell out of here before I call the cops!"

Roque surely knew he wouldn't last long in a fight with Jim, but to save face, he had to look as if it were all he could do to hold himself back. Shaking his fists, he turned and walked back to his car.

"You better watch your back, old man," he called over the roof of the car as he opened the passenger side door.

Viejo simply stood there with his arms crossed over his chest, completely unintimidated. He took a good look at the older guy behind the wheel. The guy was dark-skinned, had a bushy mustache, and had thick black eyebrows. A jagged red scar marked his left cheek, obviously the result of being on the losing end of a knife fight. His eyes were dead and dark, like an evil doll. They bore into him as the two men locked in a menacing stare. If looks could kill, the old criminal would have done the job.

Roque got into the car, spitting our curses, and the two men drove off, burning rubber as the tires spun on the asphalt. Viejo walked over to Rachel and asked her if she was okay. She said she was, but she was scared. Father Herb, Jessie, and Romero hovered around her and Isabel, offering words of comfort.

"Sorry you had to see that," Viejo said. "The Marines have zero tolerance when it comes to abusers. Sorry if I scared everybody, Father."

Father Herb, his face grim, said, "You've got nothing to be sorry about. Roque's a monster, and so is his father, Marcos, the guy driving the car. Worst of the worst."

Rachel stooped over and straightened Isabella's hair. "It's okay, honey. Daddy's gone now."

"Rachel, I don't think it would be a good idea for you to be at your place tonight," Romero said. "Roque may come looking for you. Let's go pick up some of your things, and then go to my place. You can stay with me for a while. Jim, can you help me? Father Herb, can I borrow one of the clinic's spare child seats?" She fished her key out of her purse and tossed it to Viejo. "Can you get it out and buckle it in my back seat for Isabela?"

Viejo nodded and headed for the Lexus. He extracted the seat and buckled it in behind the driver's seat. He sat up front with Romero, Rachel, and Isabela in the back. Romero said goodbye to Father Herb and pulled away from the front of the clinic.

"Damn it! I'm sorry. I wasn't thinking," Viejo said. "I didn't consider how I'd be setting up Rachel for a revenge attack from those creeps."

"That's okay, Mr. Viejo," Rachel said. "He can't do much worse to me than he usually does every day. I'm going to have to move anyway. The rent is past due. Roque promised to pay it, but he decided that buying himself a gold chain was more important. Landlord says I gotta be gone by Friday night."

"Don't worry," Romero said. "You can stay at my place as long as you need. We'll help you find someplace else to live. Someplace with security."

Viejo wondered how any man could treat the mother of his child so badly. The easy answer was that Roque was a monster, not a man. Perhaps not a monster of his own making, but a product of a horrible sub-society. With Marcos for a father, how could he have turned out any differently? Was Roque any less of a victim than the baby mamas he and his ilk preyed upon? The cycle had to be broken. His resolve to make a difference grew stronger as he looked in the rear-view mirror at the passengers in the back seat. Maybe he was meant to be here. The right man at the right place at the right time.

* * *

Romero finished putting the finishing touches on dinner. She played the image of Viejo gut punching Roque in her mind and couldn't help but smile as she remembered the creep's reaction when he suddenly came face-to-face with Jim Viejo, the ex-Marine who didn't give an inch to anybody, especially not to a wife-beating piece of crap. After the posole was piping hot, she carried a large saucepan into the dining room, where Rachel sat at the table with Isabella asleep in her lap. Georgie scampering around, delighted about all the company. Viejo came through the back door and joined them at the table.

She set the pan on the table and began to ladle the contents into bowls. She smiled at Viejo as she filled his bowl. It was different having a man seated at her table, a man like no other she'd ever known. He certainly was nothing like Howard, a nice enough guy, but he probably couldn't fight his way out of a wet paper bag.

"Sorry guys, thawed-out posole is the best I could do on short notice," she said. "It's my dad's recipe, along with my mother's Irish soda bread on the side. Nothing like a little cross-culture cuisine."

After Romero finished serving, she sat down, and everyone began to eat hungrily. She'd always loved her dad's posole, a traditional blend of thick soup made with pork, hominy, garlic, and chilies.

"I guess I don't get it, Rachel," Viejo said, wiping his chin. "You're obviously a sharp, mature young lady. How did you get into this situation? What about help from your parents?"

"Ha! Parents? What parents? All I had was my mother, who was just a more pathetic, older version of me. I never really knew which of the guys hanging around was my dad. My mom was, uh, a classic baby mama. As I got older, the guys began hitting on me. Mom didn't seem to care as long as they kept her supplied with booze and drugs. I knew I had to get out of there. Then Roque showed up, all charming and stuff."

"They always are, at first," Romero said. "They lure you in before they pounce."

Rachel sighed, nodded, and said, "Yeah, that's about the size of it. He bought me nice things. Took me out to eat at nice restaurants. He told me he was going to rescue me. What I didn't realize was that he was a recruiter, not a rescuer. He got me to move in with him. I went along with it, even when he started pimping me out. I just wanted a place where I felt safe, away from the doped-up johns hanging around my mother."

"I think we all want to feel safe and loved," Viejo said. "That's what's so sad about all this. They prey upon girls by offering safety and love to get you into their trap."

"I know," Romero said. "It's a cycle that never stops."

Rachel continued. "Of course, I got pregnant. Had to drop out of high school to take care of Isabella. You've given me a chance to escape, Renee, but after today, I'm not so sure it's going to happen."

Rachel began to sob, tears flowing. Isabel, awakened, started to cry. Rachel faked a brave smile as she hugged her daughter.

"At least you have the courage to fight back, to stand up for yourself and your daughter," Viejo said. "Where there's courage, there's possibility."

They finished the rest of the meal in relative silence, each focused on their own thoughts. After the meal, Rachel and Isabella went to bed. Viejo sat with Romero as they sipped glasses of wine in the living room. Georgie kept nudging her leg, and it suddenly occurred to Romero that she hadn't fed him.

"Oh, my god, Georgie! With all the excitement, I forgot to feed you."

"Show me where you keep his dog food, and I'll feed him for you."

"You know I feed him people food. They don't make a dog food good enough for my Georgie."

She leaned over and ruffled his short fur. The corgi licked her fingers.

"Let's finish our wine in the kitchen while I get Georgie's supper ready."

She got up from the sofa with Viejo in tow and went into the kitchen, Georgie hot on her heels.

"I couldn't help but notice how shook-up Jessica was this afternoon, like she had seen a ghost or something," Viejo said.

While Romero prepared Georgie's meal, she filled Viejo in on the pertinent details about Roque and Marcos.

"I was surprised to see the older guy driving the car was Roque's father,

Marcos. I told you Roque was the worst of the worst. His dad is the worst of the worst of the worst. Jessie's mother was one of his baby mamas. He's probably Jessie's biological father. Thirteen years ago, he raped Jessie and got her pregnant. She had Billie. Marcos is Billie's biological father, and likely his grandfather as well, which probably explains Billie's mental handicap."

"Doesn't get more messed up than that."

"Sadly, it does get more messed up than that. All the time," Romero replied. "Jessie was the only one who had the guts to stand up to Marcos. She reported the rape, pressed charges, and testified in court against Marcos. For once, the courts got it right. Marcos was sentenced to thirty-five years in the state pen. I don't know how he got out early. Might involve the cartel compromising the parole board with bribes or threats."

"Wow! That's some story."

"Roque and his ilk are an illustration of the societal problems we fight every day at the clinic. He's totally influenced by the messages he gets from his peers. Being a badass is what he idolizes, what he aspires to," Romero continued, trying not to escalate into a rant.

"The gang lifestyle is constantly being promoted as cool and revolutionarily heroic. If you don't believe me, spend a morning watching MTV. Roque thinks he has to be cool, and, in his economic and educational circumstances, cool is all he's got. He never saw role models of strong men who worked hard to support families, attend church, and teach morals. All he sees is the gang world's definition of life. These guys don't have dads in the traditional sense. Their male role models, for the most part, are the older gang guys like Marcos."

"How the world has changed since I was a kid," Viejo said. "We used to watch shows like *Father Knows Best* or *Leave it to Beaver*. TV used to provide a little vicarious parenting. There's nothing like that going on now."

"That's why you've been such an important addition to the staff. At least the kids get to see what a real man looks like. I'm so grateful you decided to join us. This whole situation stinks," Romero said, fighting the anger rising in her throat. "And I can tell you one thing for sure. Marcos being back on the scene spells big trouble for the neighborhood and the clinic. The young guys will follow him like he's some kind of Messiah.

They will buy right into his message that he is leading them in a noble rebellion against society. That the police are just pawns serving the upper class hired to keep them down. They will never embrace the truth that their problems are brought on by the choices they make for themselves."

"It's always easier to put the blame on someone else," Viejo said. "Guess that's human nature."

"It's easy to sell something if it's what the buyer wants to hear. Let's have another glass of wine and relax by thinking of easier problems, like perhaps world peace or the gradual fading of the sun."

20

Jim Viejo
PRESENT TIMES

TWO POLICE CRUISERS AND A BLACK CROWN VIC WERE parked outside the front of the clinic when Viejo arrived for work the next day. His heart sank when he saw the reason for the police presence. Every window in the entrance was shattered. Shards of glass were strewn all over the sidewalk. A giant green V was spray-painted on the front wall.

Roque, Viejo thought as he parked and got out of his SUV.

He walked over to the group of uniformed officers standing in front of the building. Father Herb was with them. He was talking to a middle-aged guy wearing a suit.

"Ah, Jim," Father Herb said when he saw him. "Meet Detectives Fermin Padilla and Landon Schumer. Detectives, this is Jim. The guy I've been telling you about."

Viejo shook their hands and asked Father Herb what happened.

"Looks pretty obvious to me," Father Herb said. "Roque wanted revenge for what happened yesterday."

"Heard you gut-punched Sanchez after he socked his girlfriend in the face," Padilla said, smiling.

"Yeah, I hit the guy. Now I'm sorry I did. Shouldn't have lost my cool like that. Now look what's happened because of it," Viejo said. He turned to Father Herb and said he was sorry.

"Not your fault. You noticed the V? That's my biggest concern. Roque's guys have had sort of a loose connection with the Vagos for a while. Looks to me like they've asked the Vagos for help."

"The Vagos are one of the worst gangs in the city," Padilla continued. "They're typical of most intercity gangs, with their urban operations thriving in barrios like this one. Drugs, primarily meth, along with prostitution. They also have a connection to the Mexican cartels, though the bigwigs stay pretty much in the background. They let the local hoods do their dirty work."

Father Herb stroked his chin as he surveyed the damage. "I'll have to call my insurance agent to see how much of this damage is covered. At least no one was hurt."

"Do you think there'll be more trouble?" Viejo asked.

"Probably," Padilla answered. "Roque didn't ask the Vagos to step in for just one hit. This is going to cost him. The Vagos will likely want a piece of his action in return for their help. I hear that Marcos is back in the neighborhood. That will be like pouring gasoline on the fire."

Father Herb sighed and shook his head. "I might have known that Roque and his guys wouldn't leave us alone for long. I thought he was too afraid to try anything with Jim around. Didn't realize he had access to seasoned thugs who would take this to a different level."

"The surveillance cameras caught the vandalism on film," Padilla said. "Five guys. All were wearing masks; impossible to identify. We all know who did it and why. Just can't prove it."

Jessie came out of the clinic with a broom and dustpan. She began to sweep up the broken glass.

"You okay, Jessie?" Viejo asked.

"No, I'm not," she sobbed, her voice barely above a whisper. "I can't believe Marcos is out of prison after what he did. I thought he was going to be there until he died."

"My guess is that he won't be out for long. His type always finds a way to screw up. We're watching him. When he makes a mistake, and he will, we'll get him," Padilla said. "The karma bus will come for Marcos, as well as for his piece of crap son. Have faith. They'll get what's coming to them."

"So, we can do nothing about this senseless attack on the clinic?" Father Herb said, turning back to Detective Padilla.

"At the moment, we can't prove anything. Pretty much have to catch them in the act before I can arrest them," Padilla replied. "Tell you what, Father Herb. I'll get dispatch to run extra late-night patrols for a while. That might deter them from trying something else. Or better yet, give us a chance to catch them in the act if they do."

Father Herb thanked him and said he had to call his insurance company and make arrangements with a window shop. Padilla asked him to give his statement to one of the uniformed officers before leaving.

"Let's make it quick. The longer this damage is unrepaired, the more frightening it will be for our kids and staff. Jim, would you stay out here and assure students and staff as they arrive that the incident is over, and it's safe to come in?"

21

Jim Viejo & Father Herb

PRESENT TIMES

TWO WEEKS HAD PASSED SINCE THE VANDALISM incident. The increased police presence had apparently prevented another incident.

Viejo knew it wouldn't last. The police department didn't have the resources to continue the extra surveillance much longer. He tried to project a sense of calm control as he went about his routine, hoping it would rub off on his students. He went to his classroom and reviewed his lesson plans before the first of the students arrived. A short time later, the kids filtered in. He greeted each one of them by name with a warm smile. Viejo knew they needed a safe space where they could focus on their math problems without the distractions of a noisy apartment and siblings who intentionally discouraged them from learning. When everyone was present, he took attendance and asked them to take out their notebooks and pencils.

"Today, we're going to learn about fractions. Can anyone define what a fraction is for us?"

No one raised their hand, of course. They lacked confidence and didn't want to be embarrassed by a wrong answer. It gratified Viejo that he'd built up enough rapport with most of them that they came to class voluntarily during the summer when they could be doing something else, most likely getting into trouble. Most of the kids really were trying to learn, like Rachel, who was fast approaching the date when she would take her GED exam. Viejo had no doubt that she'd ace it.

In the absence of a response, Viejo continued. "A fraction is a portion of a whole number. What's a whole number, you may ask? It's a one, or a two, or a three, and so on. If you have half of a one, or a third, or a fourth, that's what we call a fraction or a piece of a whole number."

Viejo could tell by the look on most of their faces that he may as well have been speaking Greek. He continued on anyway, explaining how fractions worked and why they were important. He took an apple and a paring knife out of his desk drawer.

Holding the apple aloft, he asked, "See this apple? At the moment, it is a whole apple, representing the number one." He sliced the apple through the middle. Holding up one of the pieces, he continued. "This piece is a fraction of the apple, more specifically a half." He cut one of the halved pieces in half. "Now each of these pieces is a smaller fraction. Can anybody tell me what fraction of the apple they represent?" Several of the students raised their hands and shouted, "One-fourth!"

"That wasn't so hard, was it? Math isn't all that hard when you visualize the concepts."

He spent several minutes cutting other apples into smaller segments and playing with different numerators and denominators. Most of the class was enjoying the exercise, yelling out "two-thirds" or "three-fifths" as Viejo challenged them to identify various combinations of apple portions.

Viejo noticed one of the boys wasn't participating. The boy was hunched over his desk in the back row, wearing headphones, oblivious to the lesson. Viejo walked over to where the young man was sitting and gently removed the headphones.

"You're here to learn, Roberto, not to listen to music," Viejo said, his tone nonjudgmental in an effort to be reassuring, not critical.

"Might as well hear some tunes. I can't get this math stuff. I just keep making mistakes."

"Don't think about them as mistakes. Think of them as learning steps. Ever watch a baby learning to walk? He falls on his butt most of the time, right? But he keeps getting up and trying and trying. Eventually, he learns to walk, which becomes very useful in his life. Same thing with math. You just keep trying and learning from mistakes until you get it. Math becomes useful as you go through life. You'll soon see that it was worth the effort to master the basics."

Roberto didn't look so sure, but he agreed to concentrate on the lesson instead of zoning out to the tunes on his iPhone.

"After class, I can give you some one-on-one help with today's math problems," Viejo said.

The rest of the time in class passed uneventfully, and the next math class arrived right on time. This one was for preteen girls.

"Okay, class. Before we start on our math work, does anyone remember what we learned from yesterday's life lesson?"

One of the girls raised her hand.

"I do! You read the first line of that famous book." She paused and put on an ominous voice. "'It was the best of times, and it was the worst of times.' You told us you didn't know if we were living in the best of times, given all the modern inventions or if we were living in the worst of times, in view of all the pollution and weapons of mass destruction. But you said you were sure we were living in the *only* time we were going to get, so we had better make the best of it."

"Very good, Carlotta! I'm glad to see you recalled the lesson. I hope you take it to heart and do the best you can with the time you have been given."

Father Herb sauntered in and smiled at everyone. "And what are we learning today, young ladies?" he asked.

Sonya, the deaf twin, signed to her sister, Gracie. Gracie raised her hand and said, "That we shouldn't date the guys who are hanging out on the street selling drugs and pimping. We should find guys who are at church or in school. Mr. Viejo says if you fish in a cesspool, all you'll catch are crappy guys."

All the girls giggled. Herb gave Viejo a what-the-hell look.

"I shudder to ask, but is there anything else on the lesson plan today?" Father Herb asked.

Another little girl piped up. "Yeah, Mr. Viejo says that nothing good happens after ten o'clock at night. All that bad stuff you hear on the news usually happens after ten o'clock. So, if you are home in bed, it doesn't happen to you!"

Viejo beamed with pride as Herb shook his head in mock disbelief.

"Mr. Viejo, I thought this was supposed to be a math class!" Father Herb said, pretending to be upset.

"I'm getting there; I always like to throw in some life lessons along with the math," he said. He turned to address the class. "Can anyone tell Father Herb how this relates to last week's discussion about ratios and decimals? How about you, Sonya?"

Gracie signed the question to Sonya. She signed her response. Smiling brightly, Gracie verbalized Sonya's answer.

"Suppose there are twelve girls and only four bad boys. It works out to three point three-three girls per bad guy!"

Herb laughed and said, "Well, I suppose that's one way to look at it. I'm not sure that's the way a math question will be phrased on the standard GED test, but I guess the principle is the same. Carry on, Mr. Viejo!"

* * *

Father Herb left the classroom and headed down the hall toward his office. As he walked, he reflected on how blessed the clinic was to have Jim Viejo. Mixing math with life lessons. Showing the kids how to set goals and achieve them. Keeping Roque and his gang at bay. Jim was becoming a surrogate father to many of the kids. Kids who so desperately needed someone like him in their lives.

Jim Viejo

PRESENT TIMES

As he had done almost every night since the vandalism attack on the clinic, Viejo sat patiently, hidden in a chair next to the broken first-floor window in a vacant building across the street from the clinic. He'd pulled some sniper duty during his tenure with the Marines, learning that patience was as important as marksmanship. The trick was to calm your mind without dozing off and take it to another plane, where time didn't seem to pass so slowly. He'd parked his SUV in the lot behind the building to keep it out of sight. It would only be a matter of time before Roque and his thugs returned to do more damage. Probably sooner rather than later. He felt the heft of his Beretta M9 semiautomatic pistol in the holster strapped to his left hip, hoping he wouldn't have to use it. Responding to violence with more violence went directly against what the clinic was trying to accomplish in the neighborhood.

As he lingered alone with his thoughts in the early morning darkness, his mind drifted to recollections about his life in the Marines. Did he miss it? Not really. The Corps still contributed to his identity and his sense of self, but it no longer was the be-all and end-all in his reality. Just the same, he had to admit that he'd experienced some remarkable adventures—his combat exploits during Desert Storm and again with Operation Desert Shield.

He'd served as a major with the 2nd Marine Division, a low rank, considering he'd already put in twenty-three years. In reflection, he knew it was mostly his fault. His temper and stubbornness hadn't set well with his superior officers. He thought about the time his unit was among those charged with the task of breaching a fortified berm that ran along the Saudi-Kuwait border as the major ground assault began early on the morning of February 24, 1991, in what later would be dubbed the one-hundred-hour war. He'd felt excitement as his troops moved out. The sound of artillery fire had filled the night air, and bright yellow and orange flashes of light marked the locations where the rounds were targeted.

The Marines had moved quickly into no-man's land amid explosions that made Viejo's ears ring. Huge Abrams tanks forced through the barbed wire, avoiding tank traps, although some tripped buried landmines. Marine infantry fanned out and fought to cross two obstacle belts designed to slow the forward assault.

Although the Republican Guard was no match for coalition forces, some units put up stiff resistance. As always, when in combat, Viejo feared for the lives of his men. There were going to be casualties, and his job was to keep them at a minimum. The unmistakable sound of an incoming artillery round caused him to look hard left just as the shell landed close to his position. The shockwave knocked him to the ground, and shrapnel tore into his body armor, also grazing his cheek and neck.

Jeez, that was close, he thought, getting back on his feet.

"You okay, Major?" his first lieutenant asked.

"Yeah, just a few scratches," he said, relieved that the shell hadn't landed any closer. "Come on, let's go! We got that second berm to take!"

All in all, twenty-four Marines were killed in action during Operation

Desert Storm, and ninety-two were wounded. During air and ground operations, coalition forces destroyed more than 3,000 tanks, 1,400 armored personnel carriers, and 2,200 artillery pieces. Viejo didn't need official statistics to see just how badly the Iraqi forces were beaten. He was proud of the part his unit had played in the success.

Returning to the present, Viejo checked his watch. The hours were passing slowly, and he wondered if he was wasting his time.

Fighting back fatigue, Viejo stood up from his chair and stretched, yawning deeply. He debated about whether he should quit for the night and go back to the casita for some much-needed shuteye.

Just a few more minutes, he thought, checking his watch for the zillionth time.

As he sat back down, he heard the rumble of a car engine and tires hissing on the dew-dampened asphalt. The sound grew louder. Seconds later, a black Chevy stopped in front of the clinic. Four guys jumped out. All wore masks. A big guy with a build much like Roque's walked to the trunk of his ride, opened it, and hauled out a red, five-gallon gas can. He walked briskly toward the clinic.

Viejo rushed out of the vacant building, his gun in hand, and ran across the street.

"Freeze!" he shouted. "Hands up! Get down on the ground!"

The big guy didn't hesitate. He spun around and threw the gas can at Viejo, who dodged it. The jug hit the pavement nearby and slid to a stop.

"I said freeze!" he shouted again, knowing they wouldn't, regardless of the pistol pointed at them.

Sure enough, they all ran to the car, got in, and sped off, fishtailing as the driver tried to maintain control. It was too dark to read the license number. Viejo holstered his weapon and picked up the gas can. It was full. He unscrewed the cap, and the pungent, strong odor of gasoline whiffed up to his nose.

Talk about escalating, he thought, feeling furious that he'd let them get away.

Even so, he felt grateful the encounter had not escalated into a gunfight. He had hoped to nab one or more of them for the police. Scaring them away would just convince them to switch tactics. He walked behind the vacant building with the gas can, put it in the trunk of his SUV, and got behind the driver's seat. He fired up the engine and pulled away from the vacant building. Over the many weeks he'd worked at the clinic, he'd gotten to know the surrounding streets fairly well. He also knew the location of prime hangouts for the young thugs, thanks to Detective Padilla. He cruised around the neighborhood, eyes alert for any sign of the black Chevy he'd seen in front of the clinic.

He slowed down near the park where Romero used to play as a child. The trees created a cloak of darkness, broken only by bright orange security lights around open areas near the street. He saw a group of men, blatantly smoking weed, seated on a bench. Thugs, just not Roque's thugs. He looked for the Chevy but didn't see it.

"Time to call it quits," he said, turning for home. "This'll all keep until tomorrow."

23

Jim Viejo
PRESENT TIMES

FOR THE FIRST TIME SINCE HE'D MET THE MAN, VIEJO saw Father Herb lose his composure. The priest scowled as he sat behind the desk in his office, speaking to Detective Padilla. Viejo, seated next to the detective, had just finished recounting the events of the previous night. He stated that he knew it was Roque because he recognized the black Chevy, but it was too dark to get the tag number.

"Looks like things are getting more serious," Father Herb growled. "That monster was going to burn down the clinic, and he just might have succeeded if it wasn't for Jim. You have to get him off the street, Fermin. Arrest him and his gang." Turning to Viejo, he said, "It's a good thing you followed your gut instinct, Jim. We could have lost everything if you weren't here last night."

Father Herb turned to Detective Padilla. "Arson is a whole different world than the vandalism. A fire could have spread to other properties. People could have been killed!"

"We have the same problem we did before," Padilla responded, shaking his head. "I know it's frustrating as hell, but the cameras didn't catch anything useful, and Mr. Viejo—"

"Please, call me Jim."

"Right. Anyway, we can't prove it was Roque carrying the gas can. I'll have the lab run it for prints. Maybe we'll get lucky. If we can prove it was Roque with the gasoline, it'll put him at the scene. Along with your testimony, I will have grounds for an arrest."

Viejo seethed along with Father Herb.

"Could you see if they were wearing gloves in addition to the masks?" Detective Davies asked.

Viejo shook his head no. "Too dark. If they were smart, they'd have worn gloves."

"Since when are bangers smart," Father Herb said. "Good idea about the prints. Maybe that'll be a way to stop Roque. He'll certainly be in the system for a probable match if he wasn't wearing gloves."

"They aren't particularly smart, but they know about fingerprints. I'll bet they were wearing gloves. Roque and his gang aren't going to stop," Padilla said. "Your clinic is gaining momentum. It's bound to cut into their illegal businesses. Expect more trouble. Unfortunately, the police can't do anything unless we catch them in the act of committing a crime."

"Well, you might not be able to, but I certainly can," Viejo said, anger clouding his judgment.

Detective Padilla gave him a stern look. "I don't want to hear that, Jim. We don't condone vigilantism here in Albuquerque. You might get killed or charged with a crime yourself. Leave the matter to us."

"It's a free country. I can go talk to Roque. Suggest that he check out his health insurance."

Father Herb looked uncomfortable. "God doesn't want you to resort to violence. A violent response from us would undo a lot of our good work. For now, just stay away from Roque and his dad. I'll pray about this. God will provide the answer in due time. He always does."

The meeting continued for a few more minutes, Viejo blowing off steam and the other two men cautioning him against going after Roque. Detective Padilla left, promising to increase patrols in the area for as long as his budget would allow.

Viejo went to teach his first class of the day, appropriately enough, a self-defense course for teen girls. He figured if they learned the basics of self-defense, they might be able to fight off an abuser or rapist. At the very least, the class helped build their self-confidence.

24

Renee Romero

PRESENT TIMES

R OMERO GLANCED OVER AT VIEJO AS HE HIKED NEXT to her near the timberline in the Sandias. It was a Sunday, and they'd planned the excursion for when she knew they'd both be free of other obligations. She felt mildly guilty for lying to Howard when he wanted to get together for dinner later that evening, telling him she wasn't feeling well. He sounded disappointed, but he said he understood. The mild guilt was trumped by the rush she felt being with a man considerably more intriguing than Howard. Jim Viejo was kind, gentle, caring, and tough, all at the same time. On the downside, he certainly had his demons to fight. He'd admitted he had a problem with valium, and she'd been delighted when he told her he'd flushed the pills down the toilet.

"How are you coping with the withdrawal symptoms?" she asked, highly concerned. "I know most people need rehab to get past their addictions."

"Good days and bad days, but I'm handling it. Gradually, there are more good days than bad days. Managed to cut way back on the vodka as well. Working at the clinic has been as good for me as it has been for the kids. After years of doubting God's existence, I've started praying again. Father Herb has rekindled my faith, leading me down a better path. No one has to tell you that there is something special about Father Herb. It's like he is on a whole different spiritual level than anyone I've ever met. He can be profound and yet simple at the same time. We had a helpful session a couple of weeks ago that really helped me work through some issues. He talked about paradoxical situations. You know such as, why bad things happen to good people. Non-believers use these as primary evidence that God doesn't exist. Father Herb explained there are things we are not supposed to understand at our human level but will be made clear when we ascend to a higher level. Only by faith can we deal with these situations. We need to view paradoxical situations as faith testers rather than as deal breakers in our relationship with God."

She smiled at that, leaned over, and gave him a tender kiss on the lips. "I'm so glad, Jim," she whispered. "This has been an incredible two-way street. You are a blessing to the clinic, and Father Herb is a blessing to you."

The views from the trail were spectacular at this elevation, over nine-thousand feet above sea level. Each time he took the tram to the top, Viejo was awed by the spectacular vista, featuring the shiny meandering band of the Rio Grande as it wound through the valley, as well as high desert buttes and mesas to the west that seemed to stretch out forever. A cool, invigorating breeze created the perfect temperature for a hike.

She thought about their several previous sort-of dates. They'd all been non-romantic, although she was well aware of a slowly developing sexual tension. She didn't want to move too quickly. Despite the progress Jim had made, it was obvious he was still on somewhat shaky emotional ground. She was becoming more and more convinced that she and Viejo might have a romantic future together. Compared to her experience with her cheating ex-husband, she found Jim refreshingly honest and sincere. He was certainly more interesting than Howard. When he talked about Betti, how he still thought he could feel her presence whenever he went near her music box, it didn't bother her. Just the opposite, in fact. She could see how much he still loved her, and she considered that as a plus, indicative of a man who at heart was an old-fashioned romantic.

"You're awfully quiet," Viejo said, pausing to catch his breath. "Something on your mind?"

"I was thinking about giving Howard back his ring," Romero said, surprised at herself. She'd thought it before, but she'd never verbalized it.

"Really? Why? Nothing to do with me, I hope."

"No, nothing to do with you," she lied. "Just another step in my effort to get my life unstuck from where it was for all those years. Resigning my judgeship was the first step. Volunteering more time at the clinic and increasing my class load at the law school were the next steps. I think the next logical step is moving on from a relationship I know should never go any further. I just want to move on to something new, a life that generates new experiences and creates some excitement."

They began hiking again, both keeping silent. She wondered if she should keep up the pretense or lay her cards on the table. Just as she had that thought, he said, "I know we've talked about you feeling stuck and wanting to get unstuck, but are you sure you want to throw away a relationship you've had for almost two years?" Viejo asked.

His concern pleased her. "I haven't made up my mind yet."

"Good. It is never wise to rush into big decisions. Take time to think things through before you act. Not that I'm any kind of authority on romantic relationships. I only had one in my entire life, and Betti was basically driving the bus. I didn't have a clue about what to do; I was just thankful to be on the bus!"

She considered this. Yes, she had felt disconnected from Howard for several months now, and she was ready to move on. She didn't need to give the matter all that much more thought, but she told herself she would take her time to be sure she was doing the right thing. There was no hurry, after all. Howard wasn't going anywhere.

"I have to say I've enjoyed, am enjoying, the time I spend with you at the clinic and just hanging out together after work," Romero said. "I'd be lying if I said I didn't."

Viejo smiled broadly, stopped, and gave her a gentle hug, then he kissed her.

A wave of desire flowed through her like an electrical charge. Her passion built, and she deepened the kiss. The wind tousled her auburn hair, blowing it across his face. She savored his taste, his masculine smell, and she wanted him right there and then. Of course, she knew that was impossible and that she shouldn't move too quickly for fear of ruining a good thing. But she felt the way she did, and there was no denying it.

He stepped back from her. She saw uncertainty in his eyes.

"Was that a mistake?" he asked.

"I don't think so," she said. "I liked it. Maybe more than I should have."

A slow smile formed, lighting up his face. His brown eyes sparkled and danced with mischief and definite passion. In the bright sunlight with the deep blue sky as a backdrop, he looked incredibly rugged and handsome, like the he-man he teased about being back when he first agreed to volunteer at the clinic.

"I'm glad," he said. "Now, what do we do?"

His question puzzled her for a moment until she realized he wasn't asking about the moment, but the bigger picture. Now that their mutual feelings had been exposed, where did she want this to go?

"I'm not really sure," she said. "No need for us to make any decisions right now, anyway. Let's just understand we both like each other. A lot. And see what happens next. Sound like a plan?"

"Sounds like a plan to not have an actual plan . . . works for me!"

Romero laughed. They continued hiking in companionable silence along the ridgeline, exchanging unimportant small talk about such things as the weather and the presidential election, which was starting to really heat up as George W. Bush and Senator John Kerry duked it out on the national stage. Clouds gathered to the west, darkening the sky. Romero knew the signs. Thunderstorms rolled in quickly from the west. Uneasy about being exposed at high altitudes if a fast-moving squall blew through, she stopped hiking and took Viejo by the hand.

"I think we should get back," she said. "Looks like we're going to get a thunderstorm."

Viejo scanned the sky, his face drawn in a frown. "Yeah, looks like you're right. Let's get off the mountain."

They picked up the pace as they backtracked along the ridgeline.

Several spur trails led to connecting trails below, but they were still a mile or so away. Romero became increasingly nervous as the clouds swirled and darkened. The sky took on the hue of bruised skin, bordering on greenish yellow. A jagged fork of lightning seared downward through the clouds. She gasped and jumped at the sound of the thunderclap, which immediately followed, indicating the storm cell was approaching fast.

"Come on, Renee!" Viejo yelled. "We gotta make a run for it!"

She agreed, picking up the pace. The last thing she wanted was for them to get caught on a ridgeline in the middle of a nasty thunderstorm. The danger of being struck by lightning would be greatly reduced once they reached the heavily treed area below. They struggled to balance speed with caution. A misstep could lead to a serious fall on the rugged trail.

The first drops of rain splatted on the rocks beneath their feet, darkening the trail in front of them with big, wet splotches. More lightning seared the sky, and thunder rumbled around them.

"I don't like the look of this!" Viejo shouted, barely audible over the wind. "We could be fried any second!"

"Try not to think about it. Just focus on not slipping!" Romero shouted back.

"There's the spur!" she yelled, pointing at a trail marker leading to a path downward.

"Yeah! None too soon!"

They began the descent. The grade was steep enough to force them to go down on their backsides, using their hands to steady themselves on the way down. The rain increased, soon coming down in torrents, cutting visibility to almost zero.

"Careful, Renee!" he shouted as he slid downward across a craggy rock face. "It's getting slicker by the second."

She nodded, gritted her teeth, and focused on maintaining her balance. The air smelled heavily of lightning-created ozone. Scrub pine and underbrush began to fill in the vast swaths of bare rock, and, to her great relief, they reached the relative safety of a tree-filled hollow just as a bolt of lightning struck the mountain, only yards away from where they had been just minutes earlier. Jim's decision to slide down the rock faces rather than scramble around them had likely saved their lives.

Trembling with fear and feeling the chill of the rain, she hugged herself to get warm. He stepped close to her again. Slowly, he drew close to her, his face inches away. The wind roared through the trees, whooshing loudly in the gusts. Suddenly, she felt a wave of calm submerge her fright. He cocked his head and gently kissed her on the lips, filling her with a desire she welcomed but feared. She wrapped both arms around his neck and let the passion take over. She could feel his passion as he pressed close and lost himself in her. The power of the moment was unlike anything she had felt in years. They remained in the embrace long after the kiss ended.

"This is all going too fast," he whispered in her ear. "And I don't care."

Barely able to speak, she said, "I don't either."

They kissed again and separated.

"First the balloon crash and now the lightning! Never a dull moment with you, lady!"

"Don't tell me our big, tough Colonel Viejo was actually scared?"

Maybe a little in the balloon. But the lightning? Naw. I've never worried about lightning. It only travels at the speed of light, about 186,000 miles per second. I can usually dodge it if I see it coming."

"I think I know bullshit when I hear it."

"Yeah, and if that lightning had struck any closer, you may have smelled a little of it. Let's get out of here before I get another opportunity to prove how unafraid I am when it comes to lightning!"

25

Jim Viejo
PRESENT TIMES

V IEJO GRINNED AS HE WATCHED BILLY DOING JUMPING jacks on the athletic field with the phys ed class. Tall and muscular for a twelve-year-old, Billy had begged to join the teen group, saying he was too strong to play with students his own age. Dubious at first, Viejo had finally agreed to let him participate if he could keep up with the older guys. So far, Billy had exceeded expectations. His limitations were more than made up for by his enthusiasm.

"Okay, class! Now drop and gimme twenty!"

Billy smiled at Viejo as he wiped the sweat from his forehead with the back of his right forearm. He used his T-shirt to mop his face, then dropped and began doing pushups with the rest of the boys. Viejo took great pride in the progress Billy was making. When he first met the boy,

Billy came off as shy and introverted. Little by little, he'd grown more comfortable around Viejo. Billy especially needed a good male role model, and Viejo didn't mind playing the part.

Out of the corner of his right eye, he saw an older Hispanic man walking toward them across the athletic field. He noticed the man was wearing clothes more appropriate for an office than the streets. Something about the guy looked familiar, and as he drew closer, Viejo realized with alarm that it was Marcos Sanchez.

This can't be good, he thought, wishing he had his sidearm.

Viejo waited for Marcos. He looked downright scary with that jagged red scar on his left cheek, his bushy black mustache, and his eyebrows giving him an almost feral appearance. Viejo noticed the kids had stopped exercising and gotten to their feet. Billy looked like he was about to run away. He cowered behind one of the bigger kids.

Marcos stopped about three feet away from Viejo. He kept both hands in his pockets. Viejo wondered if he was armed, his mind racing to form a plan to protect the kids.

"You're a dead man," Marcos said, keeping his voice low. "The cops arrested Roque last night on the charge of attempted arson."

"Yeah, I know. Dumbass should have worn gloves. What's it to me?"

"You a witness."

"Yeah, that's right."

Marcos took a step closer. "You disappear, and there's no case. You get that, right? You're the key to him getting locked up or going free."

"He should've thought twice before trying to burn the clinic down."

"He didn't try to burn the clinic down."

"Yeah, he did. If I hadn't been there, he would have gotten the job done. As far as your threats go, you can do your worst. I'm not afraid of you, your scumbag son, or your entire sorry crew. I'm gonna testify against Roque and have him put away for a long, long time."

Marcos took another step closer, pulling his clenched fists from his pockets. It looked like he was about to attack.

"I wouldn't if I were you. If you want to get physical, one of us will enjoy it a lot more than the other. I'm betting it won't be you!"

Marcos moved around Viejo and advanced toward the kids. The kids moved back, looking scared.

"Billy boy!" Marcos cooed as if he was talking to an infant. "How's my Billy boy doing? Do you like it here at the clinic? You like being close to your mama all day long?"

Billy continued to hide behind the big kid in front of him.

"Okay, that's enough," Viejo said, stepping in front of Marcos. "You best get going before you get hurt."

Marcos turned toward Viejo, got right in his face, and said, "Watch your back, man. This isn't over. Not by a long shot."

"Good advice to watch my back; a worthless piece of crap like you wouldn't have the guts to attack from the front. Bring it on. I'm looking forward to it!"

Viejo stood with both hands on his hips as he watched Marcos turn around and swagger away.

This ain't over is right, Viejo thought. *I should talk to Father Herb and Renee about ramping up our security.*

"Tha, that wuz my *abuelo,*" Billy stuttered. "Bad man. Mom says to stay away from him."

That stopped Viejo cold. How could Billy know he was related to Marcos? Marcos had been in prison for Billy's entire life, and Billy's father wasn't exactly on speaking terms with Jessie, whom he'd raped thirteen years earlier, according to Romero, resulting in Billy's birth. He made a mental note to ask Jessie about this when class was over.

"Your mom's right about both things, Billy. He's a bad man, and yes, you should stay away from him. Far away."

"He scares me," Billy said. "Scares Mommy too."

"I know. He scares a lot of people, but you and your mom don't have to worry about him or Roque. I've got it handled. Trust me. They won't bother you."

Billy didn't look so sure. Figuring it was best to get the class going again, Viejo told Billy to return to his row.

"Who thinks they can keep up with me around the track?" he challenged. "Let's go!"

As he ran with the kids, he thought about how much his life had changed since April. A few short months ago, he didn't think his life was worth living. He was likely destined for an ugly and early death, possibly by his own hand or as a result of an overdose of valium.

Now, his life had purpose and meaning through his work at the clinic, along with the life-changing insights he had gained from Father Herb's counseling. The most surprising turn of events was he had a new woman in his life after five long years of self-inflicted, grief-filled celibacy. Where the relationship was going and whether it would thrive or end, he didn't know. He just knew he was happy for the first time in a long time. He was gaining faith that God was leading him out of the darkness.

He thought about Betti and pictured her in his mind. Her beautiful, warm smile, her wavy blonde hair, her sparkling blue eyes. He could hear her voice in his head, soft and soothing, always supportive. He thought about her last request, urging him to let her go. The feelings of guilt still popped up occasionally, and he wondered if they always would. Whenever he went near Betti's music box, he continued to feel her presence. It was as if she could talk to him in his thoughts, and the messages he received from her made him feel like he was doing the right thing in his pursuit of Renee. He hoped the resonating with Betti was real and not something he had manufactured to justify his feelings for Renee.

26

Renee Romero

PRESENT TIMES

GEORGIE WAS STRAINING AT HIS LEASH, PULLING Romero up the steps to the clinic. After teaching an early class on campus, she'd decided to bring the dog to the clinic. Georgie was popular with the kids, especially the younger ones.

Jessica smiled brightly as they passed her desk. "Hi Georgie! How's my favorite incorrigible corgi?"

Georgie stopped, anticipating and receiving his customary ear massage.

"You might want to stop by Father Herb's office. Rachel's in there with Mr. Viejo, sharing some good news."

"Good news? What's up?"

"Don't want to spoil the surprise. Best if you hear it from her."

Romero led Georgie down to Father Herb's office, entering without bothering to knock. Father Herb, Viejo, and Rachel were sitting around the desk.

"What's up? Heard it was good news."

Father Herb turned to Rachel, beaming. "Rachel just received her GED diploma in the mail this morning!"

Rachel stood up and handed the diploma to Romero.

"Rachel, this is so great! I'm amazed at how quickly you passed all the classes with As in almost every one of them. I'm going to call the Hummer Law Firm and tell them you're ready to start next week. This weekend, I'm going to take you shopping for some office-appropriate clothes. But first, this calls for a celebration! Tell you what. I'll spring for lunch. Let's go over to Pepitos. It's within walking distance, and Georgie loves their caldo."

As city regulations wouldn't allow Georgie to eat inside the restaurant, they opted for a table on the outside patio. The air was cool and refreshing, carrying the enticing aroma of the home-style Mexican food selections. Georgie wolfed down his bowl of caldo as the others enjoyed enchiladas with sides of frijoles. Most of the conversation was a lively speculation about how bright the future was going to be for Rachel. Not used to being the center of attention, she tried with mixed success to keep her composure.

"I appreciate all the praise, but this is just as much about you, maybe more than it is about me. There's no way I could be here today without Father Herb's vision to start the clinic and without Renee leading me to the clinic and providing encouragement and support every step of the way, as well as Mr. Viejo's efforts to keep us safe. I owe so much to all of you. I know the only way I can ever repay everyone is to make a success of myself, to serve as an example to the other girls. That's what I promise I'm going to do!"

"Jim, you really saved the day or, er, the night when you stopped Roque," Father Herb said. "When he goes to trial and gets convicted, he won't be able to bother us anymore. You are a guardian angel."

"Thought angels were generally a little more attractive."

"You're plenty attractive enough for me," Romero said, knowing their budding romance was no secret at the clinic. "I . . . I mean in a certain light, of course."

"Probably pretty close to pitch dark, I'm guessing."

Everyone laughed.

"I can't believe you ordered the okra at lunch," Viejo said.

"Why? I love okra," Romero said.

"Okra? Ugh, that's got to be the slimiest food in the world. How can you stand it?"

"It's healthy. Just think of it as being vegetarian *menudo.* Slides right down."

"Bet you wouldn't feed it to Georgie."

"Bet she would," Rachael said.

"Speaking of Georgie," Viejo said. "I've been giving some serious thought to—"

"About how to save the world one Catholic clinic at a time?" Romero said, interrupting Viejo.

"No, something far more serious than that. I've been pondering why there isn't a dog food good enough for Georgie."

"And just what have you come up with, Colonel?"

"Well, Your Honor, I'm thinking that maybe the problem isn't with the quality of the dog food itself. Maybe the problem is just in how it's being presented," Viejo said. "Most of the canned stuff is horse meat, is it not? Maybe instead of the low-class names they have for it, they could make it acceptable to you dog food snobs by spicing up the names. Name it after famous horses. You know, like Seattle Stew, or perhaps Can-o-War might work."

"Maybe Trigger Treats, or Pie Ho Silver instead?" Father Herb offered, playing along.

Romero laughed and continued to tease. "How about My Food Flicka as a possibility?"

"Or Mister Ed . I. Ble?" Rachel ventured. "I used to love watching that show on one of the oldies channels."

Romero laughed along with the rest of them. She saw that Rachel was obviously proud she came up with that one. "Good job, Rachel! If this legal assistant gig doesn't work out, maybe you could do standup at the dog pound," Viejo said, chuckling along with the others.

"Very funny," Rachael said. "I don't think I'd be very good in front of a crowd. Too shy."

Romero smiled and play-punched Rachael on the left shoulder. "You don't know that, honey. You're just starting out in life. You're still learning who you are as a person. For all you know, you could have the talent of a rock star hiding inside you, waiting to come out."

"That's right, Rachael," Father Herb said. "We all have innate talents, something we're uniquely good at. The trick to leading a happy life is finding what it is we love to do most in this world and then going out and doing it. Most who fail do so because they're too scared to leave their comfort zones. They want everything to stay the same for safety's sake. Real success almost always happens outside of the comfort zone."

"Wow!" Viejo said with a laugh. "Very profound, Father Herb. You have a way of looking at the world that's uniquely you. Is that your talent?"

"Part of it," Father Herb said with a sly smile.

They arrived back at the clinic. Romero said her goodbyes, got in her Lexus, and headed off to teach her afternoon law class.

27

Jim Viejo
PRESENT TIMES

VIEJO SAT AT HIS DESK IN THE TINY, SPARSELY FURNISHED office across the hall from Father Herb's. Jessie had just left his office after delivering some disturbing news. Marcos had shown up at her apartment on Sunday afternoon, demanding to see Billy. She refused to let him in and threatened to call the police if he didn't leave immediately. He tried unsuccessfully to kick in the door, then left with an angry promise that he'd be back again soon. She was concerned that he might show up when Billy was home by himself and convince Billy to let him in. The thought terrified her.

"Billy's deathly afraid of Marcos, but he's so easily confused. Marcos could likely make up a story that would convince Billy to let him in. No telling what could happen once he had Billy to himself. I was so sure I'd never have to deal with Marcos again. I don't have a plan for him to be back in our lives."

"First thing, I'm going to ask Renee to use her courthouse connections to get a judge to streamline issuing a restraining order preventing Marcos from getting near you or Billy. Given his history, that shouldn't be a problem. Ask your landlord to put on a stronger lock. Every time you leave Billy, remind him strongly not to even go to the door to answer a knock. Marcos could use one of his people, probably one of his girls, to entice Billy to open the door. I can stay with Billy when necessary. I'd love to see the look on that bastard's face when he knocks on the door and comes face-to-face with me instead of Billy. And I'd love to provide a vigorous citizen's enforcement of the restraining order."

Viejo turned his attention back to grading math tests. Hearing a rap on the doorjamb, he looked up and was surprised to see Louis Saucedo standing tall in the doorway, sporting a big grin. The young man was wearing a new polo shirt with freshly pressed khaki slacks. It's hard to imagine this was the same sloppily dressed young man who had refused to do pushups just a few short months ago.

"Hey, Louis! Great to see you! Come in. Sit down. Take a load off."

Saucedo offered Viejo his hand. The two shook hands, and Louis sat down across from Viejo. He folded his hands in his lap.

"What can I do for you?" Viejo asked.

"I just wanted to thank you in person for everything you did for me," Louis replied. "What you, Father Herb, Ms. Romero, Jessie . . . all of you have done for me. If it weren't for you pushing me hard physically to get my GED, I wouldn't be heading out to Recruit Depot San Diego in a couple of days."

Viejo smiled at Louis with pride, soaking in the satisfaction from the young man's transformation. After getting expelled from high school, his single-parent mother forced him to attend the clinic while she pursued her GED at the clinic and worked evenings at the local Dollar Store. He'd dutifully attended but didn't put out much effort.

Desperate for help, Ms. Saucedo scheduled a meeting with Viejo. She'd told him Louis had been a bright, happy boy until two years ago when her husband suddenly abandoned them. Louis had changed almost overnight. He stopped caring about school, started hanging out with the wrong kind of friends, and was constantly getting into trouble. She feared he would soon become a full-fledged gangbanger if he kept going in the wrong direction.

"Mr. Viejo, I'm trying the best I can, but my son needs more. He needs a strong male role model. I can't provide that. I know he is basically good. He just needs a strong push in the right direction to turn himself around. Will you help him?"

"The fact that he still has enough respect for you to at least come here regularly tells me there is something to build on. I'm not a psychiatrist, but it appears to me that deep inside, he doesn't want to let you down. I'm going to build on this, but I'll need your help. Every time you notice even the slightest improvement in his attitude or actions, reinforce it with positive feedback. I'll do the same. The goal is for him to take the right path, but it needs to be his own choice, not just a way to get us off his back."

It worked almost exactly as planned. After some initial resistance, Louis seemed to sense that Veijo was for real, not just spewing out lame platitudes similar to those offered by his high school counselors, who rarely spent more than ten minutes with him. He began to thrive at the clinic, both in the classroom and in physical training.

"We were all happy to help, Louis. We try to bring out the best in everyone who comes here. Father Herb is fond of saying we all have hidden talents and that we just have to leave our comfort zones and take the risks required to find and develop them. I think a stint in the Marines will help you find yours."

Viejo noted the nervous look on Louis's face. "Something wrong?" he asked.

"Uh, no, not really. I'm just a little nervous about what to expect at boot camp."

"Expect to get yelled at a lot." Viejo laughed, remembering his basic training years ago before he shipped out to Vietnam on his first tour of duty in 1968. "And expect to get to know every muscle in your body because every muscle is gonna hurt like hell, even after you get in tiptop shape. They train recruits hard to sort the wheat from the chaff."

Louis looked worried. "I sometimes wonder if I have what it takes to be a Marine. At night lately, I've been having trouble sleeping because I'm afraid I may have made a mistake in joining up."

Viejo leaned back in his chair and cupped both hands behind his head. "We all doubt ourselves sometimes. That's perfectly normal. In fact, it wouldn't be normal not to be nervous about starting a brand-new life in a strange place and in a totally different culture. Trust me. We've all been there."

"Somehow, that doesn't help."

"I know. But you gotta believe in yourself. Believe that you will make it. Hell, the Marines could be a career for you. Have you thought about that?" Viejo asked.

Louis nodded. "Yeah, I've been giving that a lot of thought, too. It's not just self-doubt, you know. I'm also excited about the possibilities for my future; possibilities I didn't have before I came here and you helped me out with your connections in the Corps, along with pushing me to succeed."

"I spent thirty-six years in the Corps before I mustered out as a colonel," Viejo said, recalling the pain he'd been in until just recently. "It can be a great place to find a home professionally, as long as you know what you're in for. One of the best benefits, if you don't get killed, is the pension. You know, fewer than one in five Americans have one. Let me assure you, it's a godsend to have a steady income when you're retired."

"I never thought of pensions and stuff like that."

"Most people don't when they choose a career. They're too young to worry about things like that, but it's something I always encourage people to do when they're deciding what path to take in their lives. I know retirement is the last thing on your mind right now, but it's definitely something to consider when determining whether you want to make the Marines a lifelong career."

"You got a pension?"

"Damn right. A good one too. Have you given any thought to college? You need a degree to be an officer."

"I've been told that I'm not college material. It was hard enough studying for my GED. About drove me crazy, especially the math problems."

"Who told you that? The losers you used to hang with? That's bullshit! Never embrace bullshit. It will lead you down the wrong path, and you'll smell bad along the way."

"The Marines will provide you with an opportunity to get an education. Without one, your career, whatever it turns out to be, won't flourish the way it should. Sure, not everyone should go to college, but in today's society a degree is absolutely essential to get into high-paying positions. It's like that in the military, too."

"I think I'm more of a follower than a leader, Mr. Viejo. I never was a leader in the crowd. I tried so hard to fit in, but I didn't want to stand out. Didn't want to draw attention to myself."

"Well, there's some validity to that. There's a saying in the military: Never volunteer for anything. Truth be told, I never believed in that saying. If you don't try to be the best you can be, you'll always come up short. Don't convince yourself you can't do something before you've even tried. Don't tell yourself that you're not college or officer material when you actually don't know one way or the other. You won't know until you try."

"You're quite the cheerleader."

"Sometimes I have to be. Sometimes, you have to be your own cheerleader as well. That's something I learned a long time ago. You've only got yourself to rely on in this world. Sure, if you find someone to love and who loves you back, that person could be worthy of your trust. But the fact is we're all in this world alone, but thankfully with God as our shepherd. No denying it."

They talked for a little longer. Viejo reassured Louis that he had no doubt he would excel in the Corps. He could tell that his former student left his office feeling more confident than when he first sat down.

As Viejo went back to doing his paperwork, he heard another knock on the door. He looked up and smiled as Father Herb entered the office, his face grim and full of concern.

"What's wrong, Father Herb?"

"Fermin just called to give us a heads up. Roque Sanchez just made bail."

28

Jim Viejo
PRESENT TIMES

VIEJO TAPPED THE STEERING WHEEL OF HIS SUV TO the beat of a familiar classic rock tune, his mind on nothing in particular. He was tired after a long day of teaching and looked forward to a relaxing evening chilling out at home. Perhaps he'd visit with Renee, but he wouldn't mind some alone time. Thanks to Father Herb, the guilt-driven demons were at bay, and he was becoming comfortable in his own company. He reflected on how Betti and he had learned to deal with being separated during the times he was deployed. They'd held to the old adage that absence makes the heart grow fonder. In their case, it had proven to be true.

One of the many things he loved about Betti was her familiarity with military life. She'd grown up as a military brat, and the family would frequently pull up stakes when her father was assigned to a new duty station. Skilled at making new friends from a very early age, she brought that skill set to their marriage, viewing every relocation as an adventure and an opportunity to meet new friends.

He soon left downtown and was on his way around the mountain. The traffic was heavy for a little while, thinning out as he put more distance between himself and the city. He glanced in the rearview mirror, surprised to see the same blue 4x4 pickup he'd noticed behind him shortly after leaving the clinic. Several car lengths behind him, it steadily maintained his rate of speed.

Could these guys be from Roque's gang?

He turned off on a side street to see if the pickup stayed on his tail. It didn't. He saw it continue on its way. The two guys in the front seat didn't even glance his way as they went by. He exhaled loudly, realizing he'd experienced an adrenaline rush similar to the ones he was familiar with from his combat exploits.

You're getting paranoid in your old age, he thought, as the rush subsided. *On the other hand, a little paranoia might be a good thing.*

Roque and Marcos had both threatened to kill him. He shouldn't ignore that fact. They might not have the huevos to do it, but the Vagos likely had killers in the gang who wouldn't hesitate to take him out. Gun violence was not uncommon in their world, and the police could do little to stop it. It was like trying to put out a five-alarm fire with a squirt gun. The clinic was gaining momentum. Its positive impact could potentially go much further toward reclaiming the neighborhood than a strong police presence ever would. Eliminating him would send a message to the neighborhood that the gangs were in control and anyone trying to stop them was in severe danger.

Viejo hung a U-turn and proceeded back to the main road. He continued on toward Romero's place. He couldn't help but keep looking in the rearview mirror. No pickup. He felt a slight sense of relief but took the incident as a reminder that sooner or later, most likely sooner, the threat would be real.

He turned onto the access road and drove through the woods toward Renee's home. As he turned into the circular driveway, he noted that her Lexus was not parked outside. It could be in the garage, but she usually didn't bother parking inside. With so many sunny days all year long, the vehicle didn't need much protection from the elements. He parked, got out, locked up, and ambled down the path to the guest house, pausing in the beautiful park-like backyard. He listened to the soothing whisper of the gentle breeze in the trees, smelled the fragrant scent of the pines, and told himself that, at least for the moment, life was good. Viejo continued walking to the guest house, erasing the blue pickup incident from his mind.

29

Renee Romero

PRESENT TIMES

FRIDAY EVENING. ROMERO DREADED THE MOMENT TO come. She parked in front of Howard's favorite restaurant, wondering if the place would still make his top ten list after she gave him the bad news. She saw his car parked in a nearby spot. Typical. He was always early, never late. Howard was aggravatingly compulsive about punctuality, keeping his life as orderly and predictable as possible.

She sighed, resting both hands on the wheel, avoiding going inside. This was going to be a painful conversation for both of them. More for him, though. He wouldn't have seen this coming.

Okay, girl, she thought. *You can do this. You gotta go do this.*

She got out of the car, shouldered her purse, and reluctantly walked to the front entrance of the restaurant. She wondered if she should wait until after they ate to tell him the relationship was over and she was moving on to a new life that didn't include him. Would that be cruel to let him think everything was fine and then smack him upside the head with the painful news after they ate? She still wasn't sure of her course of action as she opened the glass door and stepped into the lobby. The hostess greeted Romero with a warm smile.

"Ah, Ms. Romero," the hostess said, "your reserved table is this way."

The hostess gestured in Howard's direction. Romero followed her to the table. She'd been hungry earlier, but she wasn't now. Her stomach was churning nervously. Howard stood, came around from the other side of the table, and gave her a quick hug and a kiss on the lips.

"You look gorgeous tonight," he said, stepping away from her.

"Uh, thanks," she said awkwardly.

They sat down. The server took their drink orders. They exchanged small talk as they looked over the familiar menu—"how was your day" and "nice weather we're having" sort of stuff. The server brought their drinks and asked if they needed more time before ordering their dinners. Renee said she wasn't quite ready, and he left, saying he'd be back soon.

"So, how's it going at the clinic?" Howard asked, taking a sip of his martini.

Setting down her glass of chardonnay, she said, "Roque Sanchez just made bail."

"You had to expect that he would. His people have plenty of money, and the charge of attempted arson isn't something big enough for a judge to deny bail."

"You don't have to tell me that. Did you forget I'm a judge?"

Howard laughed awkwardly. "Sorry, my bad. Do you think there'll be more trouble?"

"Jim thinks so. Father Herb thinks so. So does Detective Padilla," Romero replied. "Just what'll happen next is anybody's guess. But it's not going to be good. The clinic is making a difference in the neighborhood. Roque has partnered with the Vagos for more muscle."

"Can't say I'm surprised about that. Ever since Jim Viejo showed up on the scene, they're not as easily able to intimidate the kids or the staff coming into the clinic. They backed off considerably since he arrived, right?"

Romero nodded in agreement. "Yes, that's right. Having a guy like Jim around is giving Roque and his crew something to think twice about. The problem is, I think they intend to escalate. It won't end with trying to burn the clinic down. I can't tell you how lucky it was that Jim staked the clinic out the other night. If he hadn't been there—"

The waiter returned and they ordered their dinners, an Italian pasta dish for him and her favorite, the poached salmon. They sat in silence for a long moment. Howard was obviously uncomfortable. Was she giving off some sort of vibe? Could he sense something was wrong? She thought he probably could. Should she tell him now or wait? She decided to wait. Hell, she might not tell him tonight at all. Putting off the odious chore of breaking up with him did not sit well. She didn't usually procrastinate, but maybe a little more wine would help. They exchanged more small talk until the server brought their dinners, and they ate in companionable silence.

When she finished her dinner, she ordered another glass of wine and contemplated what she should do next. Finally, she took the plunge.

"Howard," she said, "I think we need to talk."

"About what?"

"About us."

"Uh-oh. That doesn't sound good," he said, shooting her a tentative smile that faded as soon as it appeared. "You're serious, aren't you?"

Romero nodded, feeling as if she were rapidly descending in a runaway elevator. "I'm afraid so," she said. "I think we should move on to date other people. We're not officially engaged, even though I'm wearing the ring you gave me last year. We don't plan to ever get married and—"

"That was your choice. You told me after your divorce experience, you didn't believe in the institution of marriage. You said you didn't think making a legal commitment through marriage was necessary if two people were truly in love. Have you changed your mind?"

"No, I haven't. It's just that I feel it's time to make changes in my life that will make a positive difference in how I feel about being alive. I've felt more alive since I quit the bench than I have in years. It's like I was asleep, and I've suddenly awakened to a bright, sunny new morning."

Howard looked like he was in shock. He appeared nervous, as if he was losing his composure.

"You don't love me anymore?" he asked, his voice barely above a whisper.

Romero wanted to tell him that was indeed the case, that she may never have loved him at all. This was a relationship of convenience, a sort of placeholder. The reality is that it was never going to evolve into anything else. She had just put up with the tepid relationship because it was easier than making the effort to find and sustain a relationship that would truly satisfy her. Jim Viejo might be exactly what she was looking for, and she was determined to see where it might lead. At her age, she couldn't afford to spend more time in a stagnant relationship with Howard.

"Do you love me?" she asked, instantly regretting the question, knowing the painful answer.

"Of course I love you. How could you ask that question? I'm asking you because you say you don't want to invest in the relationship anymore. Be honest. Have you ever loved me?"

Romero hesitated too long.

"Well, I guess that's my answer. Mind if I ask you why now?"

"I don't know what to say."

The server returned to the table and asked if they wanted to see a dessert menu.

"Just the check, please," Howard said, his tone sharp and impatient, reflecting his smoldering anger.

His reaction didn't surprise her. After all, she'd just told him they'd both been wasting their time for almost two years.

"I'm sorry, Howard."

"So am I," he said, polishing off the last of his martini. "It's Jim Viejo, isn't it? He's the reason you're walking away from me."

"No, it's not him," she lied. "He may be part of the story, but there's more going on than my meeting someone new. Like I said, I'm going through a sort of midlife crisis. I want to get unstuck. I want to reshape my life into something more meaningful, and if a relationship isn't delivering all it should, then it's time to move on. It's nothing personal."

"It sure feels personal. You're kicking me to the curb for a jarhead."

"You should have this back," she said, taking off the diamond ring he had given her a year ago and handing it to him.

He took it and put it in his pocket without saying a word. The server returned with the check. Howard removed a credit card from his wallet and placed it in the black leather sheath holding the check.

"Look, we can still be friends, right?" she asked.

Howard snorted loudly. "Yeah, sure. Like that really works. It's almost insulting, Renee. Can we still be friends? I don't think so."

She felt bad about his response, but again, she wasn't surprised. She hoped he could manage to be cordial in front of mutual friends, but given Howard's reaction, most likely not.

"I'm sorry to hear that, Howard."

The server took the check and returned a few minutes later, thanking them for choosing to dine there. Howard quickly retrieved his credit card, inserted it in his wallet, and stood up from the table, his face red with anger.

"Have a good life!" he said sarcastically and stalked out of the restaurant.

Well, you've really done it; no turning back now, she thought, gathering her purse as she stood up from the table.

As she left the restaurant, she felt oddly buoyant, as if she'd rid herself of a heavy weight on her shoulders. Taking bold steps forward was never easy for her, but experience had taught her it was generally best to deal with problems head-on and come out the other side as quickly as possible. She got into her car and drove home, eager to see Viejo and tell him she was free to pursue a relationship with him without the encumbrance of Howard lurking in the background.

Romero parked in her driveway, got out of the car, and went inside to make Georgie a gourmet hamburger for supper. The little corgi greeted her enthusiastically, as usual. She squatted down and rubbed his head as he rapidly wagged his stubby tail. The effect of the wine, coupled with the relief she felt from having the dreaded confrontation with Howard behind her, combined to make her feel slightly giddy as she prepared Georgie's dinner.

"How's my Georgie?" she squealed. "What would I ever do without you in my life?" she said as she stood up and headed into the kitchen.

"You're the best four-legged friend I have in the whole big wide world," she cooed as Georgie's excitement grew with the smell of the sizzling meat.

She fed Georgie, grabbed a bottle of wine, and walked out the back door into her garden, dimly lit by the porch light. As soon as she stepped off the back steps, her movement triggered the motion detectors installed in nearby security lights clicking on as the area lit up like a Christmas light display as she walked briskly down the path to the guest house. It gave her a sense of security knowing Viejo was staying in the guest house. It was somewhat disconcerting, living alone in the remote area. She didn't believe in owning a gun, figuring her alarm system would be sufficient to ward off intruders.

Romero smiled as she reached the front door of the guest house and pressed the doorbell button. Viejo answered a minute later.

"Renee! Fancy seeing you here!" he said with a laugh. "I see you've come bearing gifts. Come in. Come on in!"

Romero stepped inside, stood on her tiptoes, gave him a gentle and yet slightly passionate kiss on the lips.

"That was nice," he said, gesturing toward the kitchen. "Let's hang out there. I'll get a couple of glasses."

"Excellent plan, Colonel!" she said, sitting down at the kitchen table.

She felt a little nervous about telling him she'd just broken up with Howard, unsure of how he'd react. Perhaps he'd be happy about it, but she couldn't say so with certainty. Jim was hard to read. He wasn't exactly an open book.

Viejo opened the wine, brought the bottle to the table, and sat down after filling their glasses. He held his up and clinked hers.

"Cheers," he said and took a sip.

She did the same. They exchanged small talk about nothing important until she leaned back in her chair and gazed at him intently, hoping he could see the message in her eyes. Fortified by the additional wine, she took the plunge.

"I've got some important news to share with you."

Viejo raised an eyebrow, wary about where this might be heading. "And what might that be?"

She held up her left hand. "Notice anything?"

Viejo looked confused. "Should I?"

"Yes, you should." She waved her hand in front of his face. "You sure you don't see anything different?"

Romero grinned when she saw Viejo get it.

"Your ring's gone!" he said, his voice reflecting the surprise he obviously felt. "What happened? Did you lose it somewhere?"

"You could say that. I gave it back to Howard after I told him I wanted to date other people."

What she saw on Viejo's face puzzled her. "What's the matter?" she asked.

"You didn't break up with him because of me, did you?"

"Like I said on our hike, you're part of a much bigger story. Don't give yourself all the credit for the breakup. It wasn't all about you. It's about me. I just don't think Howard and I should waste any more of our time together."

"Oookay," he said, refilling his glass. "If you say so. I just don't like the idea of my wrecking someone else's relationship."

"You didn't."

"Good."

"I was thinking that you could move into the main house with me now. No need to stay separate."

Viejo frowned. "You're moving pretty fast, Renee. Why don't we take it slow for now?"

Romero didn't understand why what he said would hurt her feelings, but it did. She wondered if he really didn't love her after all. Although she knew it was right to break up with Howard, she hated to think she'd been wrong about Viejo. Nevertheless, she ventured further out onto the thin ice.

"You don't want to live with me?" she asked, fighting back her defensiveness.

"I didn't say that," Viejo said. "I just think we should go slow. Not rush into anything without giving it some thought. I also like my alone time, Renee. I've gotten used to living alone. Not sure you'd want me to live with you. I can be kind of a moody slob sometimes."

Now she was angry, not sad. "You don't like spending time with me?"

"That's not at all what I meant. Don't you value your alone time? Isn't that why you and Howard weren't living together?"

She had to admit he had a point, although it didn't diminish her hurt and anger. Why wouldn't he jump at the chance to move into the main house? It didn't make sense. She put her wineglass down on the table a little too hard. She noted the surprise on Viejo's face. It looked as if he wasn't expecting her reaction. She stood up from the table.

"I should go," she said, adding, "thought you'd be happy about the news, and we could move our relationship to the next level. Clearly, I thought wrong."

She turned away from him and walked briskly to the front door.

"Come on, Renee!" he said to her back. "Don't be that way. Let's talk this out."

She opened the front door and stormed out without saying another word.

30

Jim Viejo

PRESENT TIMES

VIEJO WAS SITTING ALONE AT HIS DESK, TRYING TO figure out how to get back on speaking terms with Renee. She was giving him the cold shoulder, obviously from the anger and embarrassment resulting from his rejection of her wine-induced proposal for him to move in with her. They hadn't exchanged a single word in the week since she stormed out of the casita. Every time he tried to explain, she turned around on her heel and walked away.

Father Herb poked his head in the door. "Mind if I come in?"

"Sure, why not? I'm not getting much done anyway."

"What's going on between you and Renee?"

Viejo sighed, wondering just how much he should tell Father Herb. He decided to come clean.

He noted Father Herb was not surprised when he heard Renee had broken up with Howard.

"I never thought those two were the real thing," Father Herb said. "Never seemed to be any spark there. Romantic relationships are complicated and often painful. I've come to believe that my vow of chastity is more of a blessing than a burden. Saves a lot of wear and tear on one's heart."

"You can say that again."

"Why didn't you want to move into the main house with her?"

Viejo had been wondering the same thing all week. He tried to put a noble spin on it, rationalizing that he was thinking of her best interests, not wanting to drag her, although willingly, into a relationship doomed to failure because he wasn't capable of being the partner she deserved. On the other hand, maybe he wasn't being noble at all, just the opposite. Perhaps he was simply cowardly, afraid to venture into unknown waters. She would have to wait, but was what he was able to offer worth waiting for?

"I think she's moving too fast."

"Did you tell her that?"

"Yeah, I did. I wish I had been thinking quickly enough to diffuse the situation and explain that I care too much about her to rush things. But I had the old deer-in-the-headlights reaction when she exploded at me. In the light of day, I think she realizes the wine affected her judgment, and she shouldn't have surprised me like that. I know she's embarrassed and using anger as a deflection, but I can't smooth things over if she won't even speak to me."

"Ah, matters of the heart," Father Herb said. "You'll never be able to figure them out because the heart isn't rational. It works on pure emotion and instinct. It's why mature people don't handle emotional issues much better than teenagers do. Give her some space. Don't crowd her. Don't try too hard to fix things. After all, your relationship with Renee isn't broken. It just hit a speed bump, is all."

Viejo hoped so. He really did like Renee Romero. Admitted to himself that he might just be falling in love with her. It appeared she loved him, although she hadn't actually told him so. He could see it reflected in her brilliant green eyes. Being loved again felt wonderful, and he didn't want to lose the feeling.

"I hope you're right, Father Herb," Viejo said. "She really is something special. I'd hate to lose her. I hope she can trust me in that our problem is only a timing issue."

"You and she will be fine. I'm sure of it," Father Herb said. "You're aware I know things about you. I know God has a plan for you. Renee might very well be a part of that plan. Have faith that everything will work out for the best. Keep reinforcing the belief. That's more than half the battle."

"Is this coming from the horse's mouth?"

Father Herb laughed. "Since I'm an avowed celibate, it might be from the other end of the horse, Jim."

"That was a rather earthy disclaimer for a priest," Viejo countered, laughing along with him.

"I've often found that a little humor, even the ribald sort, can grease the mental wheels. Why do you think God invented laughter?"

31

Jim Viejo

PRESENT TIMES

VIEJO APPROACHED THE ACCESS LANE TO ROMERO'S estate. As he turned into the lane, he noticed a black SUV slow behind him and then continue down the main road. He cursed himself. He had been distracted, thinking about how to get back into Renee's good graces. Uncharacteristically, he had neglected to check traffic behind him for a possible tail. If the black SUV had been following him, he had inadvertently shown Roque's guys where he lived.

Better check it out, he thought.

He continued down the private road at a snail's pace, parked by the side of the lane, and walked the short distance back to the main road. Keeping to the cover of the woods, he looked in both directions. Nothing. Better safe than sorry; he had to assume the worst-case scenario. They likely already knew this lane led to Renee's house but might not know that he lived on the property, as well.

Viejo trudged back to his SUV, got in, and drove to the end of the lane. He parked in the circular driveway and hesitated when he saw Romero's Lexus in its usual spot. He considered knocking on her front door to see if he could patch things up with her, but he decided to heed Father Herb's sage advice and let things simmer down. If he didn't allow a little time, his attempt at reconciliation could evolve into a confrontation they would both regret. Lines in the sand. Words that could never be retrieved. He planned to talk with her at the clinic in the morning to tell her about the possible consequences of Roque knowing that he lived on the property. Hopefully she wouldn't take it as him using it as an excuse to move away. Although he knew it was a sore subject with her, he planned to give her one of his pistols and show her how to use it. She was touchy about guns, proud that she had never owned one, and adamant about never having a gun in her home.

He strolled back to the guest house, went inside, and headed to the kitchen to open a can of tomato soup for dinner. He had never mastered the art of cooking. After Betti passed, if he wasn't eating at the officer's mess on base, he subsisted on fast-food takeout and frozen dinners. The casita was as silent as a crypt except for the gentle rustle of leaves that carried through the open kitchen window on a warm breeze. He heated the soup, got some crackers from a cabinet above the counter, crushed some into the soup, and ate straight from the pot as he sat at the kitchen table.

Viejo didn't mind the silence. Father Herb had shown him how to find a calm space where trouble didn't exist, only serenity and contentment. He had become more adept at getting into that space with practice. It was his favorite part of the day and just one of the many ways Father Herb had changed his life for the better. He reflected on the priest telling him they'd met that day on the highway because God had a special mission for him. Viejo figured that mission amounted to helping at the clinic, but he understood there could be more to it than that. There always seemed to be more when it came to Father Herb. Supernatural? Spiritual? Whatever, it was good fodder for meditation.

Viejo finished his soup, washed and dried the pot, put the spoon in the dishwasher, and poured himself a generous glass of vodka. He added water to dilute the alcohol, along with several ice cubes. He wondered if watering down the vodka was a step in the right direction or if he was simply fooling himself by faking progress. Probably a baby step, he mused. Did that old saw about *a journey of a thousand miles begins with a single step* contemplate that the first step could be a small one? He no longer intensely craved valium's mellowing effects, although the desire to pop a pill bubbled to the surface from time to time. He had not acted on the desire for several months. His dependence on alcohol was more problematic. He knew darn well that once a drunk, always a drunk, meant that to truly kick the habit, he would have to quit drinking altogether. He wasn't quite ready yet but promised himself that, eventually, he would go cold turkey.

Out on the back porch, he sipped his drink and quietly contemplated the beauty of his surroundings. The sun sank below the horizon, and darkness soon cloaked the forest. With the darkness, the natural sounds from the surrounding forest grew crisper, providing a perfect background for the evening, leading him to a comfortable drowsiness. He finished half of his drink and poured the rest out on the grass, congratulated himself for the small act of restraint, and went to bed.

32

Renee Romero
PRESENT TIMES

ROMERO RECLINED ON HER COZY COUCH, WATCHING TV with Rachael. Isabella was sound asleep in the back bedroom. The show was some sort of romantic comedy that captivated Rachael but stirred up a range of emotions in Romero. Her mind wandered incessantly back to Viejo and his rejection of her offer for him to move in with her. She had not anticipated his reluctance. It hurt her feelings, but being honest with herself, it was mostly her pride that hurt. She felt embarrassed more than anything else. *Damn that wine!* A few extra glasses, and she had thrown caution to the wind, plunging into a seize-the-moment state of euphoria, not considering how it might come as a shock to Jim. Of course, her temporarily impaired lack of judgment led to her overreaction, which in turn led to her present state of affairs with

Jim. He was simply being protective of them, not wanting to allow a spur-of-the-moment decision to lead to something he wasn't sure about. They were both old enough to know better.

How could she mend this without having to swallow too much pride? Was her pride all that important anyway? Jim would certainly understand that the whole incident was simply an alcohol-induced lack of discretion on her part, which got blown way out of proportion. Perhaps a simple apology would suffice or, better yet, just start acting as if the problem had never occurred. What was the famous line from that old *Love Story* movie? "Love means never having to say you're sorry?"

Georgie nestled in her lap and was fast asleep. She felt the warmth of his furry little body through her jeans and T-shirt. The dog gave her an immense amount of emotional comfort, especially at times like tonight. As she started to drift off, she heard something that sounded like a dog barking outside. She cocked her head and listened more intently, just to be sure. There was definitely a dog out there.

"You hear that, Rachel? Sounds like a dog barking."

"Yeah, it does sound like a dog is out there somewhere. Wonder what it's doing way out here in the middle of nowhere?"

"Your guess is as good as mine," Romero said, walking to the front door and stepping outside, Rachael right behind her. "I wonder if someone abandoned the poor thing out here?"

Romero closed the door to keep Georgie from charging out into the yard. Security lights illuminated the front of the house. At the edge of the lighted area, Romero saw a tiny shape emerge from the shadows.

"Hey, it's another corgi!" Rachael chirped, clapping her hands together delightedly.

Romero saw Rachael was correct. It was a corgi, but it was in bad shape. The dog's fur was matted in places, and bare patches of pink skin revealed spots where the fur was missing, possibly due to a close call with a bobcat. The poor little thing was obviously scared and miserable. Not wanting to approach the dog for fear it might run off, she squatted down and called to it. The dog took a tentative step toward her, then another.

"Here, little doggie!" Romero cooed. "Here, doggie, doggie! You must be starving. If you come, I'll make you a steak dinner just like I make for Georgie. Georgie's my dog. He's a corgi just like you."

"The dog doesn't know what you're saying, you know," Rachael said with a laugh.

"Yeah, I know. But dogs are sensitive to tone of voice and body language. I don't want to appear to be any sort of threat."

Romero saw the dog stiffen. It growled, low and deep from the throat. It sounded a bit ridiculous coming out of such a small animal. She wondered what was setting the dog off.

"Here, doggie, doggie! Come to mommy," Romero said.

The dog started barking and jumping up and down.

"Something's scaring it," Rachael said. "Looks like it's trying to warn us about—"

Just then, Romero saw the security lights in the backyard switch on. First one, then another. Panicking because she knew a deer wouldn't set them off in sequence like that, she gasped at the thought of an intruder being out there with them. She didn't think Viejo had set off the lights. It was unlikely he would visit unannounced, given the current chill in their relationship. She was about to stand up and rush back into the house with Rachael when the corgi ran to her. She scooped it up in her arms.

"Come on, Rachael," she said, rushing back to the front door. "Something set off the motion detectors, and it wasn't a deer. Someone's out here!"

Romero saw the fear in Rachael's eyes. Whatever was happening, it couldn't be good. She ran back inside with Rachael and closed the front door, locking it with both deadbolts. She put the dog down, noting it was female. Georgie ran to greet his new companion. The dog ignored Georgie and instead ran straight into the kitchen. Romero followed right behind, along with Rachael.

A few seconds later, she entered the kitchen. To her horror, she saw the alarm panel was dark.

"Oh, god!" Romero said. "Someone disarmed the alarm!"

"What?"

Romero looked out into the backyard and stopped cold. Marcos stood there in full view, clearly not caring if they saw him. He held a semiautomatic pistol in his right hand. He raised his arm, clasped the grip with both hands, and fired at her.

"Get down!" Romero screamed, grabbing Rachael and pulling her to the floor with her as glass rained down on them from Marcos's first round.

"Someone's shooting at us!" Rachael screamed, stating the obvious in her disbelief.

Trying to keep her cool but not succeeding, Romero said, "Yeah. It's Marcos out there. No doubt his no-good son is with him. Come on, we've got to get Isabella!"

Rachael began sobbing uncontrollably. "I don't wanna die!"

Romero guessed that neither Marcos nor Roque knew about the casita. They'd somehow found out that Viejo was staying with her and thought he was in the house with them. They were coming to get him, as promised. She crawled to the kitchen table to retrieve her cell phone. They crawled rapidly backward out of the kitchen. As soon as she got around the corner with Rachael close on her heels, she got up and ran upstairs, trying to think of what to do. She dialed 911 as they hit the stairs.

The operator answered and asked what the nature of the emergency was.

"Home invasion!" she screamed. "Armed intruders breaking into my house and shooting at me."

"Are they in the house now?"

"Not yet, but they will be any second!"

They bolted into Isabella's room. The little girl was up and sobbing, scared out of her mind at the sound of the gunfire.

Rachael ran to her daughter and lifted her into her arms. "It's okay, honey, Mommy's got you!" she whispered, trying to comfort the frightened child.

They heard the kitchen door being kicked in. It slammed open with a loud bang.

"Oh, god!" Rachael cried.

"They're in the house now!" she yelled into the phone. "They just kicked in the kitchen door!"

"Find someplace to hide until the police get there. I'm sending them now!" the operator responded. "Stay on the line."

Some place to hide? Is she kidding? Romero thought.

"Okay," she panted into the phone. "Come on, Rachael! We gotta get to the attic!"

"I know you're in here, old man!"

"Roque?" Rachael cried. "Oh, god no! Not him!"

"Time to get what's coming to you, old man!" Roque yelled, making his voice sound like a taunt.

Romero led the way to the attic. She didn't like the idea of hiding up there. They'd be trapped. But that was their only alternative. At least it was the furthest point from the kitchen. Hiding there might buy them a little more time. Marcos and Roque were searching the first floor. She ran through the attic doorway, pulling Rachel and Isabella with her. The hollow-core door and flimsy lock wouldn't be much of a deterrent.

"Help me with this!" Romero whispered. "Try not to make any noise."

Together, they gingerly pushed a heavy old dresser in front of the door, trying to be as quiet as possible. Romero's panic increased as she considered the relatively long police response time to her house. Maybe they'd be lucky, and the dispatcher could catch a county deputy on patrol in the area.

"That won't keep 'em out for long," Rachael whispered in her ear, not wanting Isabel to hear.

"Yeah, that's what I'm afraid of," Romero agreed. "I'm feeling really stupid for not having at least one gun in the house for self-defense."

33

Jim Viejo

PRESENT TIMES

V IEJO LURCHED AWAKE AND SAT BOLT UPRIGHT IN BED, unsure of what disturbed his sleep so abruptly. Instinctively, he knew something wasn't right. He leaned over and switched on the brass lamp on top of the nightstand next to the bed.

Boom! . . . Boom, boom, boom!

Gunfire? At first, Viejo didn't believe the unmistakable sound, but the loud crack of semiautomatic gunfire could not be anything other than what it was. Viejo immediately flipped into full combat mode. He dressed quickly, put on his sneakers, and grabbed his sidearm, along with two full clips from the nightstand drawer. His mind raced as he punched Romero's contact button on his cell phone. The call went straight to voicemail.

"Damn it!" Viejo growled. "Why aren't you picking up?"

Viejo dialed 911. When the operator answered, he told her he'd heard gunshots nearby.

"We have units on the way, sir," the operator said. "We got a call about a home invasion at that address just a minute or two ago. Where are you? Are you in the house with the other residents?"

"No, I'm renting the guest house on the property."

"Stay put until the police arrive."

Viejo hung up. Pocketing the cell phone, Viejo was out the front door in seconds. He ran full speed toward the main house, pumping his arms and breathing deep to get the most out of his muscular body. Romero's backyard was dark, except for the porch light showing the kitchen door smashed in and the kitchen window shot out. Viejo's heart sank. He guessed Marcos and Roque had come to pay him a nasty visit. That would explain Viejo's feeling of being followed recently. They knew where he lived, or at least they thought they did. They probably didn't know anything about the guest house and thought he was living in the main house with Romero.

Oh, God! Don't let anything bad happen to them, he thought, wondering briefly if he was strong enough to bear additional loss in his life.

Reaching the backyard, he stopped running and went into stealth mode, skirting the perimeter of the yard, keeping under cover of the shrubs as he surveyed the situation. He knew he had to get inside quickly, but he didn't want to be an easy target by rushing in through the smashed kitchen door. As he circled the house, the only car he spotted was a black Chevy, parked a short distance down the access lane. He would've bet his pension that it belonged to Marcos and Roque, but it was odd there weren't more vehicles. Was it possible the two men came alone to kill him? That would be out of character for the cowardly scumbags. He completed his recon of the exterior and concluded all the gangsters were inside, still uncertain how many there were.

"Screw it," he growled.

He sprinted to the porch and through the door with his gun drawn, safety off. Once in, he hesitated and listened intently for any sign of the intruders. There were sounds of footsteps on the second floor, two sets of them.

"Come out, come out wherever you are! Don't make me play hide and seek. I hate that game."

Viejo recognized Roque's voice, which confirmed his conclusion that the young thug and his dad were on a personal vendetta against him. They had probably decided not to bring other gang members who could someday testify against them to bargain their way out of a jam. They were probably high on drugs or booze, or they wouldn't have rushed into the house so brazenly, where they surely knew Viejo would be armed and capable of putting up a helluva fight.

"We know you're all in here somewhere!" Marcos shouted. "Your cars are parked right outside. Come face the music, Viejo. It's over for you! It's over for your girlfriend!"

That's what you think, dirtbag, Viejo thought as he climbed the stairs to the second floor.

*   *   *

Sweat soaked Romero's T-shirt. Her heart pounded so hard in her chest that it beat a steady drum in her ears. She fought to stay rational. Rachael cowered in the corner, trying to keep Isabella quiet. Two floors down, the dogs barked furiously.

Boom! . . . Boom, boom, boom!

Oh, no! Georgie! They're shooting at the dogs! she thought in mounting panic.

The barking stopped. Romero sobbed in grief. She listened in horror to the sound of doors opening and closing one floor below. It would only be a matter of time before they came up to check the attic out.

"They're on the second floor," she whispered to the 911 operator.

"Where are you and the other two residents?"

"We're in the attic. We've propped a dresser against the door, but it won't stop them for long! Where the hell are the cops?" Romero asked, fighting not to scream at the operator.

"They're still ten minutes out. Stay quiet and calm. Got anything else to add behind the dresser?"

"Nothing that would help much."

"Stand to the side of the door. They'll likely try to shoot through it."

Suddenly, she heard barking on the other side of the attic door.

"Oh, God! It's the dogs!" Rachael whined. "They'll lead them straight to us."

Relieved the dogs were still alive but scared about them leading the bad guys to the attic door, Romero switched off the lights and sat on the floor in front of the dresser, ignoring the dispatcher's advice. Maybe if she used her weight and strength, they wouldn't be able to get through the door. She knew they'd have no problem killing her and Rachael. Dispatching a three-year-old was not beyond them either. They couldn't leave witnesses.

No, no, no! she thought as the barking intensified. She knew it was only a matter of minutes now before they would be at the door. The police would be too late. She closed her eyes and prayed, realizing she might not have much longer to live. *God forgive me! I thought I was offering Rachael and Isabella a safe haven. Instead, I foolishly brought them out here, miles away from police protection and without a single weapon to defend ourselves.* She wondered where Viejo was. Had he heard the shots? He was their only hope, but he was outnumbered. Would he only be another victim?

* * *

Viejo swore under his breath as he dashed up the remaining stairs. He heard dogs barking. Why two of them? He heard footsteps ascending the attic stairs on a run.

"Shit," he whispered, realizing it was the gangsters heading for the attic. That would be the logical place for Romero and her guests to hide.

* * *

Romero whispered into the phone, telling the 911 operator that the intruders were at the attic door.

Thud, thud, thud!

Roque and his father kicked the door.

Romero wondered if bullets could penetrate through both the door and the dresser.

"Come out now!" Marcos screamed. "We won't hurt Judge Romero.

We only want you."

Did they know Rachael and Isabella were with her? Not that it mattered now.

Boom!

Another gunshot. The doorknob disintegrated and then came the thud of more violent kicks.

"Oh, God!" Rachael cried. "This can't be happening!"

* * *

Viejo reached the bottom of the attic stairs just as Roque fired another round into the door.

"Freeze!" he screamed. "Drop the guns!"

The men spun around and fired at Viejo. He felt the first bullet pass close to his left cheek and a stabbing pain started in his right side above the waist. Reacting instantly, he fired back, aiming for center mass. His first round hit Roque square in the heart, dropping him instantly at the top of the landing. His second round hit Marcos in the right shoulder, hurling him backward against the wall, causing him to drop his weapon. He clutched the wound and howled in pain. The dogs stopped barking and cowered in a far corner.

"I ... I ... thought you were in there," Marcos stuttered.

"Well, I wasn't, dumbass. Did you know Rachael and Isabella are in there with Renee? Would you have killed them as well?"

He merely glared, an answer in itself.

"You sick son of a bitch! I guess it doesn't matter to a monster who would kill his own granddaughter, but do you care that you're the reason your son's dead? I pulled the trigger, but you're the reason it ended this way. What chance did he have with a piece of crap like you for a father? Too bad it wasn't you who died tonight. There still might have been a chance for Roque to turn his life around without you in the picture."

Marcos had no reply. Any remorse he might have felt was well hidden behind his mask of unfiltered hatred as his dark eyes glared at Viejo. He leaned against the wall and slowly sank into a sitting position as he lost consciousness. Blood oozed from his wounded shoulder, streaming into the larger trail from Roque's body. The pungent odor of cordite filled the hallway.

Viejo heard sirens approaching, a lot of them. He ran up the remaining stairs, retrieved both weapons, and stuck them in his belt.

"Renee! Renee!" he screamed, pounding on the door. "You okay? Everyone okay in there?"

He heard her call to him from behind the door.

"Is it safe to come out?"

"Yeah, I got both of 'em. And the cops just arrived."

She opened the door and stepped into the hall, her trembling increasing as she surveyed the gory scene. She flew into his arms and squeezed him tight. He could smell the fear on her clothes as they clung to each other. She felt a warm wetness soaking into her shirt. She stepped back from him and screamed, "Oh, my God! You've been shot!"

She stared, seemingly in shock, as she looked at the red splotch of blood on her T-shirt.

Viejo somehow managed to change his grimace into a smile. "Just a flesh wound. Had much worse. I've been putting pressure on it and got the bleeding stopped, but I'm gonna need stitches."

They heard a bullhorn telling everyone to come out the front door with their hands up.

"I better go open that door, or they'll break it down," Viejo said, hurrying down the stairs.

He shouted to the police on the other side of the door that the situation was contained and that he was a resident, not one of the intruders. He put all the guns on the table in the foyer, including his own, and opened the door. A small army of sheriff's deputies and city police were outside, fanned out in the yard. Blue lights flashed in the night, radios crackling with an exchange of voices and hissing with static.

Viejo raised both hands. "I'm one of the ones who called 911," he told the lieutenant in charge. "Heard gunshots. Went to investigate. Ended up killing one and wounding the other after they fired on me."

"You've been shot," the lieutenant observed.

"It's not as bad as it looks. I've already stopped the bleeding."

"An ambulance should be here any minute. Get you taken care of. What's your name?"

Viejo gave him his name and restated what had happened, including that one intruder was dead and the other one needed an ambulance. The lieutenant asked a deputy to order an additional ambulance. He contacted the dispatcher and asked her to arrange for someone from the coroner's office to accompany the crime scene team.

"I'll need all of you to come down to headquarters to give your statements. I realize it's late, but it's best to do it as soon as possible while the details are still fresh in everyone's minds. It is probably a good idea to have the women come down now so they can give their statements while you're being patched up at the hospital. I'll call the emergency room to alert them to take you in for treatment as soon as you arrive, so it shouldn't take long."

Viejo thanked him, realizing because of Renee's status, the lieutenant was having them go to headquarters instead of staying where they'd all been traumatized. He turned to go back into the house just as Renee, Rachel, and Isabella were being led down the stairs by two female deputies. Renee was trying to comfort Rachael, who was crying uncontrollably.

"Roque's dead," she sobbed. "I can't believe it! I hated him but always prayed that he would go to prison and not be killed! Oh God, he would have killed all of us, even his own daughter!"

The lieutenant strolled over to the sofa and stared at a bullet hole. "What do you suppose they were shooting at?" he asked, stroking his chin. "Sofas aren't dangerous."

Viejo examined the hole. There were no burn marks around the edge, so the round was fired from at least several feet away. Then it dawned on him. "I think they were trying to shoot the dogs," Viejo said.

"They were. It was terrible," Romero said, scooping Georgie up in her arms. The other corgi licked her left ankle. "But they may have bought us some time by distracting them for a few minutes. Turns out, it was all the time we needed."

The lieutenant laughed when he saw the corgis. "You mean to say they tried to shoot those little things? Not much of a threat, if you ask me."

"They most likely wanted to kill the dogs just out of pure meanness," Renee spat. "If you do a blood sample, I'll bet you'll find they were high on something, or else they never would have had the courage to come out here with just the two of them. Even brains the size of theirs would have realized that Jim wasn't an easy target."

Romero put the corgis in the car, along with Rachel and Isabella. They followed the lieutenant to police headquarters. On the way, she called a friend who agreed to keep Rachel and Isabella for as long as it took to get her house back in order.

* * *

The emergency room visit didn't take long. Viejo was whisked back to a treatment room as soon as he arrived. The doctor had been advised of the nature of his wound and had everything he needed laid out and ready to start. He cleaned the wound, applied an antibiotic, and finished stitching and bandaging in less than fifteen minutes. He offered Viejo a bottle of painkillers. Viejo refused, telling the doctor, "I can get along without those. Pills and I are not exactly pals."

When he arrived at police headquarters, Renee and Racheal had already finished giving their statements and were waiting for him outside the interview room. He gave his statement and was rising to leave with Renee and Rachel when Detective Fermin Padilla came through the door.

"Well, Jim," he said. "Looks like you had quite the night."

"He saved my life," Romero said. "He saved three lives tonight. I'm sure they would've killed us if they'd gotten through that door."

"You won't face any charges for what happened," Padilla speculated. "Clear case of self-defense. You're a pretty good shot, if I do say so myself."

"Thanks," Viejo said. "Did a stint as a firearms instructor. I usually hit what I aim at."

"Apparently so. Then why is Marcos still walking this mortal coil?"

"Roque fell into him just as I fired," Viejo said. "The son accidentally saved his father's life. Too bad it wasn't the other way around."

"I'd have to agree," Padilla said. "I called Father Herb. He's on his way here." He turned to Renee. "Father Herb said you could both stay at his place tonight. The crime scene investigators will be at your house for the rest of the night. If they finish before you get up, I'll make sure an officer is present to secure the place until you can arrange for a contractor to temporarily secure the kitchen door and window."

"Thanks for calling Father Herb, Fermin," Romero said. "I don't think I could take a hotel right now."

"Me either," Viejo said, flinching at the pain in his side. "A little late to get a room, anyway."

"You could sleep tonight?" Romero asked, incredulous. "I'm so wired I could stay up for a week!"

Viejo knew the scenario all too well. When the adrenaline rush wore off, which it would soon, she'd crash fast. He didn't bother to tell her, though. He figured she'd find out soon enough on her own.

"Marcos is being held in police custody overnight at the hospital," Padilla said. "His wound isn't severe. The bullet missed all the important stuff. Too bad. It would have saved the state a lot of money if you had killed the bastard. He's lucky to be alive. "

"I wouldn't exactly say so," Viejo said. "Might have been luckier for him if he had died."

"Yeah, the rest of his life isn't going to be a piece of cake, sitting in prison with nothing but a bunch of rotten memories. He's been arrested and will be charged with three counts of attempted murder in the first degree, along with a bunch of lesser charges. There's no way he gets out before he dies. Thanks to you."

"Glad to hear it."

"Great to have those guys off the street for good," Romero said. "Maybe this will influence the rest of the thugs to quit harassing the clinic."

Father Herb rushed in, looking haggard and worried.

"You guys okay?" he asked. "I about passed out when Fermin told me what happened. Had to rush right down here to make sure you're okay."

"Yeah, I'm okay," Viejo said. "Just a flesh wound. You should see the other guys."

Father Herb didn't laugh. "You all had a close call tonight. I thank Jesus that you are all still alive!"

"Things might've been much different," Romero said, "if Jim hadn't shown up when he did. Came just in the nick of time." Romero reached over and gave Viejo's right hand a quick squeeze. "Jim was my knight in shining armor."

"Shiny or not, a little armor would have been helpful. Maybe I should keep a set in my closet for the next time," Viejo joked, uncomfortable with being called a hero.

"Jim, do you think you should call Mary Jane to let her know what happened?"

"No use waking her and Peyton up at this hour. They would probably want to rush out of the house to check on us. At this point, there's really nothing for them to worry about. I'll call them early in the morning before they have a chance to hear about it on the news."

"Well," Detective Padilla said, "I'm sure you all want to get going. We're done here for now. I'll let you know if I have additional questions. All seems pretty clear to me, though."

Viejo yawned. "Yeah, I'm pretty tired and still wired, though. Like you, Renee, but I couldn't stay up for a week."

Father Herb looked at his watch. "Wow, it's late. I'm used to getting up about this time, not turning in."

They stood up, said their goodnights, and left the conference room. Viejo held Romero's hand as they walked to her Lexus. Neither of them said anything. They didn't have to. The harrowing experience brought them closer together, wiping away any residual chill in the relationship. Father Herb told them to follow him to his house. "You shouldn't have any trouble keeping up with my old truck."

* * *

Viejo opened the passenger side door of Romero's Lexus to the sound of both corgis barking their greetings. He hoped Father Herb wouldn't mind having the dogs as well. He got in and buckled up. Romero did the same and followed Father Herb's truck out of the parking lot.

"Boy, that's one beat-up dog," he said, nodding toward the stray corgi. "Looks like it's been—"

"She," Romero corrected. "The dog is not an it. She's a she."

"Point taken," Viejo said, shooting her a sideways grin. "But you gotta admit the dog looks like she needs to see a vet."

"I plan to take her in for a checkup and her shots. After that, a trip to the groomer. I'm also planning to keep her as a playmate for Georgie. Don't know how she got to my place when she did, but I think God must have sent her to warn us that Marcos and Roque were about to attack."

Viejo considered that as food for thought. Maybe a topic for conversation with Father Herb. The main thing was, everyone got through the ordeal relatively unscathed, except for the bad guys.

A short time later, Romero parked behind Father Herb's truck in the driveway of a modest adobe home in a middle-class neighborhood.

"Looks like a nice enough place," Viejo observed as he unbuckled his seatbelt and opened the car door.

"Yeah, the private funders of the clinic subsidize the rent here. As you know, the church proper doesn't contribute to the clinic."

They got out of the car, each carrying a corgi, and followed Father Herb to the front door. He let them in and showed them around. Romero noticed a package of dog food on the kitchen counter.

Looking at Father Herb, he said, "Dog food? How did you know we would have dogs? Do you know something about this that we didn't?"

"I know lots of things you don't know, but it's too late for a discussion tonight. Let's just go with priestly intuition for now. I'm afraid you'll have to take the couch, Jim. I only have one guest room."

"That's fine with me. I just need a blanket and a pillow."

"I can arrange that," Father Herb said. He turned to Romero and said, "I've got a travel toiletry kit you can use to wash up. Come on, I'll show you to your room."

After Father Herb set them up with their sleeping arrangements, he said, "Help yourself to anything in the fridge if you're hungry. There's some red wine in there too. Now, if you don't mind, I'm off to bed."

He headed for his bedroom, leaving Viejo and Romero alone. The two dogs were already asleep on their makeshift bed of old blankets. Viejo thought he'd feel more tired than he did. Killing a man and wounding another wasn't something he took lightly. He had replayed the events of the evening over and over again since leaving the police station. He couldn't find a reason to feel guilty about what he had done. His actions saved lives. In his view, those lives were much more precious than the ones he had taken. Talking it through with Father Herb would likely reinforce his lack of remorse. He thought the wine might help him sleep.

He hugged Renee. "How about a glass or three of the good father's wine?"

"Helluva an idea. I hope he's got more than one bottle in the fridge."

Viejo went into the kitchen with Romero. She opened the cabinets and found two wine glasses while Viejo opened the screw-top wine. With their glasses full, they walked out to the back patio and sat down. The evening air was slightly chilly, but more invigorating than uncomfortable. The slightest hint of dawn revealed the coming day in pale blue in the sky to the east over the Sandias. Stars still shone brightly to the dark west, and a fingernail-sized white moon was visible as well.

Romero sipped her wine. "I don't know how I'm going to react to what happened. That was so traumatizing. Will there be some residual effects, flashbacks, things like that?"

"Wouldn't be surprised. You'll probably have nightmares for a while. That's normal. Don't let them worry you too much. You may experience some mood swings as well. Possibly some irritability. All normal."

"Thanks for letting me know. I just keep seeing Roque's blood-soaked body sprawled out on the landing. God, there was a lot of blood."

"Getting shot in the heart tends to make people bleed a lot."

"Apparently," she replied, impervious to Viejo's weak attempt at gallows humor. She reached over and took his hand in hers. "I'm not sure I even want to go back to the house. Who's gonna clean up the mess? There's so much blood everywhere."

She let go of his hand and exhaled loudly.

"Fermin told me he knows some crime-scene cleaners. They specialize in gruesome situations that other cleaners won't touch. I'll get them started as soon as the crime scene investigators are through. Once they're done, we can deal with a contractor to fix all the physical damage. In a couple of weeks, your house won't show any sign of what happened.'

"Who'd have ever thought that I would have to deal with cleaning up after a shooting?"

Viejo reached over and took her hand in his, reveling in the warmth of her touch and the smoothness of her skin. He loved the sound of her voice and the way she smelled. They remained silent as they finished their wine. The rising sun, still below the horizon, painted the sky light orange and transformed the high clouds into balls of white puffs. A wave of peace washed over him. He'd come so close to losing her. He couldn't imagine not having her in his life. She would never be Betti, but Betti would want him to have a completely new relationship, not a substitution for herself. He had sensed something unexplainably special about Renee since their first non-date at the pub. The feeling had grown stronger, as if somehow Betti were behind this, operating with whatever mysterious powers departed souls might possess.

He decided to venture onto thin ice.

"Renee," he asked, his voice tentative, "do you still want me to move in with you?"

She leaned over and kissed him tenderly on the lips. "Now, Colonel Jim Viejo, what do you think? But bring your guns with you. I've had a serious change of heart relative to home protection."

Epilogue

T WO YEARS HAD PASSED SINCE VIEJO FIRST ARRIVED in Albuquerque, desperately needing another direction for his life. It had been a struggle for him at first, but with the help of his family, Father Herb, and Renee Romero, he was able to claw free from the demons that had been torturing him since the deaths of his wife and son. He'd found his way back to faith as well, and with that acceptance of Christ as his savior came the peace and serenity he had all but forgotten. The satisfaction he felt from his work at the clinic had been wonderfully therapeutic. The old priest had been right. Helping others was a powerful way to help yourself.

With Roque dead and Marcos in prison serving three consecutive twenty-year sentences for attempted first-degree murder, along with a host of other charges, the gang activity around the clinic decreased, and the direct intimidation of clients and staff stopped altogether. The new leaders of the gang took the path of least resistance, steering clear of the clinic and retired Marine Colonel Jim Viejo. The number of kids the clinic served increased dramatically as word got around that the clinic was a safe place for the little ones and teens, and especially the baby mamas. Viejo was still somewhat mystified by Father Herb. *Was the guy just an incredibly intuitive human or some kind of angel?*

Father Herb had invited Viejo to his office on a late Friday afternoon for a glass of wine to celebrate Jim's second anniversary at the clinic.

As they sat and chatted, Father Herb finally said, "The big guy upstairs is pleased with you, Jim. He told me to give you his blessings."

"He couldn't bless me Himself?"

Father Herb laughed. "Oh, no. God doesn't work like that. It's not time for your face-to-face meeting. Hopefully, not for a good many years to come!"

"I'm very, very okay with that," Viejo said, laughing. "Everybody wants to go to heaven, but nobody wants to go tonight! You took me on as a project, and I suspect you're not done with me yet. You're probably going to keep trying to get more light out of my twenty-watt bulb."

"Bingo! Whoops, that was a little over-the-top Catholic!"

* * *

Viejo's romance with Romero had matured to the point where neither had doubts about a permanent commitment. When he asked Romero if she would marry him, she said yes without hesitation. They planned a simple wedding in the small chapel at the clinic, with only family and close friends invited. Of course, Father Herb was the celebrant. It seemed only fitting that Meghan would be the maid of honor, as she was happy to take full credit for bringing the couple together.

The reception was held in a field outside the city under a big white tent. Romero's repaired balloon, and the chase crew stood by to send Viejo and Romero aloft on their first flight as a married couple. The balloon stood ready to go, its giant rainbow canopy straining at the tethers being manned by the twins, who had become experienced crew members over the past two years.

After the final toast and numerous well wishes from the wedding guests, Viejo turned to Romero as they stood next to the basket. He leaned in and kissed her gently on the cheek again, not wanting the moment to pass. He straightened a loose strand of her auburn hair.

"You ready to go somewhere over the rainbow with me?" he asked.

She nodded. "Till death do us part, Colonel."

"Glad to hear it. Back at you. Let's go. The crowd's getting restless."

He climbed into the basket and helped Romero get in. It wasn't easy trying not to tear her wedding dress, but they managed. Father Herb stood next to the basket with a big grin on his face.

"You look like two little kids in a candy store," he said, laughing.

Viejo beamed at Father Herb. "That's sorta how I feel."

"You're about to embark on a new voyage through life, one you both deserve." Father Herb continued, saying, "God wants you to be happy. Let go of the ghosts from the past in both of your lives. Look to the future with faith in God's love and kindness, His generosity, and His ability to help you make positive changes in your lives, as well as in the lives of others. I'm so happy for you both."

Viejo's heart felt full, almost as if it was about to burst with love for Renee, life, and the world at large. How different things were just two years ago. This couldn't be merely coincidental. Too many moving parts.

He leaned close to the priest's face. "Are you ever going to tell me what or who you really are?"

"Not going to happen. The essential part of the mysteries of faith is that they are, indeed, mysterious. If they weren't, faith wouldn't be required, and faith is the key to everything."

"Thank you, Father Herb," Viejo said. "Thank you for everything you've done for us."

"I had lots of help," he replied, pointing upward.

Romero shouted to her chase crew that they were ready for takeoff. The crew untied the anchor lines from the stakes driven into the ground near the basket. Viejo felt the balloon lift gently up from the ground and slowly move forward in the breeze as Romero goosed the burner, sending bright blue and orange flames up into the mouth of the envelope, heating the air inside to create additional lift. Romero put her arm around his waist and pulled him close.

"You're all mine now," she whispered.

"Glad to know."

They ascended higher and higher until the people below looked more like ants gathered around Matchbox cars. The patchwork grid of various crops painted the ground in squares of green and brown. Buildings looked like dollhouses. To the west, the vast high desert stretched as far as the eye could see, and to the east, the beautiful Sandia Mountains dominated the brilliant blue sky.

Viejo thought it was time. He turned to Romero and said, "I think we're up high enough now."

Romero nodded, her face suddenly serious.

Viejo stooped over and picked up Betti's music box. He could feel her presence strongly. He sensed joy and happiness in her spirit.

"I'll always love you, Betti," he whispered. "You know that, right? You'll always have a special place in my heart, and I know you're glad I've found new love with Renee. I know you want me to be happy, and with your blessing, I am."

He wound up the music box, and "Somewhere Over the Rainbow" sounded sweet notes into the clear air. A single tear trickled down his cheek as he opened the box and looked at the gray ash that once was his beloved Betti.

Romero put her arms around him and hugged him close. "It's time to set her free, Jim," she said.

At that, Viejo leaned over the edge of the basket on the leeward side. He turned the music box upside down, releasing a gray cloud that suddenly and inexplicably turned into a golden glittering whirlwind, spinning next to the basket, keeping pace with the balloon's forward progress.

Viejo couldn't believe his eyes. Was this Betti's spirit? Had she been with him all along, watching over him like a guardian angel?

"Betti?" Viejo asked.

The glittery cloud spun faster and shot upward toward the heavens.

"She's free now," Viejo said.

"Yes," Romero said, kissing him gently on the lips, "and so are we!"

JOE S. BULLOCK has been a banker for more than forty years and has managed several institutions. He currently resides with his wife and a variety of loveable dogs in Los Cruces, New Mexico.

His first novel, *Walking with Herb*, won numerous national awards and was adapted into a major motion picture of the same title. You can find the book wherever books are sold.